"THERE ISN'T A MAN IN ENGLAND OR ON THE CONTINENT WHO WOULD NOT BE HAPPY TO SET SELINA UP AS HIS MISTRESS."

"She would never consent to such a thing," said his wife. "You are all about in your head. First you are talking about getting her in to one of Prinny's gatherings. Next you will be talking about getting her into Prinny's bed!"

Her husband chortled. "That's exactly the thing. The whole world knows what a lover of beauty is our Prince Regent. He will think Selina a treasure beyond compare, and she will be adored by him as Nell Gwyn was by Charles the Second." He kissed his wife again, this time on the cheek. "That is exactly the thing! Selina will be a mistress to the Regent."

Fawcett Books by
Helen Tucker:

A MISTRESS TO THE REGENT

A STRANGE AND ILL-STARRED MARRIAGE

A MISTRESS
to the
REGENT

Helen Tucker

FAWCETT COVENTRY • NEW YORK

A MISTRESS TO THE REGENT

Published by Fawcett Coventry Books, a unit of CBS Publications, the Consumer Publishing Division of CBS Inc.

Copyright © 1980 by Helen Tucker

ISBN: 0-449-50027-6

Printed in the United States of America

First Fawcett Coventry Printing: February 1980

10   9   8   7   6   5   4   3   2   1

For

EDGAR ESTES FOLK

One

"He is not the man I would have chosen for her," Flavian Curtis said in a confidential tone to his wife, Daisy, "but I suppose he will do well enough, even though he is an untitled foreigner and scarcely a month older than Selina. At least he comes from a family of substance and is presentable in the polite world."

Daisy glanced toward the stairs to be sure her niece was not on the way down before answering. "If it must be a foreigner, I wish he could be French instead of Italian."

"My dear gel, have you forgotten that we are at war with the French? It would not do at all for Selina to marry a Frenchman now." Flavian's eyebrows went up slightly as they always did when Daisy uttered what he considered one of her tottyheaded statements. A rather small woman of voluptuous proportions, Daisy had what Flavian called soulful brown eyes. Her blond hair was beginning to be flecked with gray, which made her appear even blonder, but when Flavian called her lightheaded he

7

was, in an affectionate way, referring to what was inside her head rather than the color of her hair.

"No, of course I haven't forgotten that we are at war with the French," she answered quickly, "but somehow the French don't seem quite as foreign as the Italians."

"That is only because Italy is farther away," Flavian explained, "and because you speak a smattering of French and not one blithering word of Italian."

"Oh, yes I do," she replied, her tone becoming slightly argumentative. "I have learned *grazie* and *come sta* from Carlo. And there he is now," she added, hearing the great knocker thump on the front door. "What reason shall I give him today for answering the door myself? Our mythical servants should be quite recovered from their various maladies now."

"Simply tell him that they have *not* recovered yet," Flavian said. "Never mind, I shall answer the door myself and make whatever excuse comes first to mind."

He knew Daisy did not mean those occasional remarks as barbs to stab him, but they always did. Perhaps he was too sensitive about his meager means, about not being able to provide for her and her niece the way a well-off gentleman would, but, all things considered, he thought he had done fairly well. He had an amazing amount of self-confidence which, he was aware, came from his appearance rather than from being born of the gentility or from an ability to earn a vast fortune. A portly man, he was of striking appearance with his salt and pepper hair, rugged features and erect bearing. He could easily have passed for a lord, a baron, or even a marquess, and the bane of his life had always been that he was none of these.

When Selina Bryand had come to live with them two

years ago—just after her eighteenth birthday—he had managed (and he never let Daisy know how) to move from shabby Bulton Street to fashionable Half Moon Street so that the girl would have a better chance of luring suitable beaux to call upon her and—it was to be hoped—eventually offer for her.

And call upon her they had—handsome, ugly, rich, not so rich, titled, and untitled—for Selina was an extraordinarily beautiful girl. Her parents (her mother was Daisy's only sister) had been killed in a tragic accident when a runaway horse had caused their carriage to overturn five years ago. Although there was not much money, there had been enough to keep Selina at Miss Travis' Select Academy for Females for three years. Then, when the money gave out, Selina had been sent to London to live with her aunt and uncle-in-law. The girl, Flavian had noted with glee, could make a most advantageous marriage because of her superb beauty, poise, and disposition. But, unfortunately, an early offer from the kind of man both Flavian and Daisy wanted for her was not forthcoming because she lacked the one thing that would assure her of this: a dowry, preferably a large dowry but, failing that, even a small one. Selina came to them with not a feather to fly with, and Flavian decided that only with his wits and her beauty could a proper trap be baited and proper game be caught.

Now, he opened the front door to the proper game which had been caught in that trap, the only man who, in two years, had met the requirements of wealth, position in the world, and social acceptability: Carlo Moraldo.

Young Moraldo, on his own, had not much to recommend him, Flavian admitted, except his good looks—he was handsome in a rather ethereal way, reminding Flavian of some fragile poet—but he was the nephew of Aldo Barelli, the Italian artist who, though he had no title, was very plump in the pocket and was welcome anywhere in London that he might choose to go, including Carlton House. (It was even rumored that he might some day do a portrait of Prinny.) Therefore, his nephew was more than welcome at the small but astonishingly ornate house in Half Moon Street.

"Good evening, sir," the trapped game said respectfully, remembering Selina's uncle's early words to him to "speak English, for God's sake, when you are among English-speaking people," and this before Carlo had uttered one word to Flavian in *any* language. He was, therefore, more than surprised when Flavian jovially slapped him on the back, then shook his hand and said cheerily, "*Buona sera,* Carlo. *Buona sera* indeed!"

It did not occur to Carlo that these were the only words of Italian which Flavian knew and that he had learned them just for tonight, a very special occasion.

"That confounded butler is still out," Flavian said conversationally, appearing to be in good humor despite domestic disaster, "and so are two of the maidservants. I suppose . . ." he shrugged dramatically, "we should consider ourselves most fortunate that the three of us have not come down with the epizootics also." Certainly that was a disease the young Italian had never heard of.

"The epizootics, sir?" Carlo Moraldo looked at the older man questioningly. "But is that not a disease of animals?"

"Come in here," Flavian said quickly, leading the way into the drawing room where Daisy sat as close to the big fireplace as it was possible to get without scorching face and hair. "I will tell Selina you have arrived." He went toward the staircase muttering in a tone just loud enough to be heard across the room, "Drat those maids anyway! I shall never get used to being inconvenienced thusly."

Daisy smiled at Carlo, but more at her husband's words, knowing that never in his forty-five years or in her forty-three had either of them ever had a servant to wait upon them except when they had been fortunate enough to visit in homes where servants were employed. "Is it bitterly cold out?" she asked Carlo.

"Indeed, yes, and I think snow is threatening. Strange weather for so late in the season when we should be seeing signs of spring."

"Then perhaps you should not keep Selina out too late," she said. "No longer than necessary for the . . . the social amenities," she added quickly. She did not want anything—not *anything* at *all*—to go amiss this evening, but she did want Selina home as soon as possible so the girl could tell them in great detail everything about Carlo's family—his uncle and sister whom Selina was to meet for the first time—and the house in which they lived.

Daisy and Flavian had hired a hackney-carriage to drive them past the house in Grosvenor Square where Aldo Barelli had lived, with his niece and nephew, for nearly a year, and they had been impressed, not only by the address, but also by the simple elegance of the mansion. It was at least three times the size of their house in Half Moon Street and they were sure, although they could not see behind the house, that there probably was a coach house in back which also would have been larger than their home. (They had a small carriage house, but it had always remained empty because, as Flavian said, "Even if

11

I could afford to buy a horse he would certainly starve because I can't afford to feed another mouth.")

It was on the day that they saw the house in Grosvenor Square that Daisy and Falvian decided that Carlo, who already had declared his intentions, would be a suitable match for Selina. They began to treat him with more courteousness then, even deference, when he came to call. It worked out just as they hoped it would, for within a week Carlo had offered for Selina's hand in marriage.

Consequently, tonight marked the culmination of two years of frantic planning and fervid play-acting on the part of the Curtises: Selina was to be taken to the grand house in Grosvenor Square to meet her prospective in-laws for the first time, Carlo's sister, Gemma Moraldo, and their uncle, the noted Aldo Barelli.

Above stairs, Flavian knocked at Selina's door and went in immediately at her bidding to enter. Even though he was so accustomed to her beauty by now that he hardly ever remarked it, he gave a quick intake of breath as he saw her standing in front of the long mirror on the wardrobe door and turning slowly, as though studying herself and her gown critically from every angle. She looked to him more like a vision than something real and of this world. Her brown hair was done up in a Greek knot, thereby accentuating her lovely face with its delicate features and large brown eyes. Her expression was one of intense animation and expectation, as though she knew every next moment would be the most joyful and most memorable of her life. She looked almost beatific, Flavian thought.

She was wearing a new gown of water-green silk which had been made just for this occasion. Flavian had been willing to part with the money, an enormous amount, because Daisy had insisted that "this will be the most important gown she will ever have."

"More important than a wedding gown?" he had asked, amazed.

"Of course," Daisy had said, "for unless she makes a good impression upon Carlo's relatives, there will be no wedding."

So Flavian had managed to come up with the money to employ a dressmaker of the *ton* for the occasion. (And he had chalked it up in his mind, as though marking upon a blackboard, as another sum spent in an investment which he hoped would soon pay off a handsome return.)

Looking at the investment now, he was sure that it had been worth every shilling he had spent. The bodice fit snugly, showing off beautifully both the buxomness and the slim waist. The skirt flared from the bodice and contained velvet bows of a darker, contrasting green. The total effect of girl and gown was breathtaking, Flavian decided. It was quite enough to render the already love-sick, tongue-tied Carlo completely speechless.

"Do you think I look all right?" Selina asked. "Not too overdone for what Carlo says will be a quiet family dinner?"

"You'll do very well," Flavian said, thinking understatement would add less to her nervousness than to be told the truth: that she was the most stunningly gorgeous sight upon which he had ever clapped his optics! The truth, he thought, might cause her to be self-conscious, and that, in turn, might cause her to make mistakes that would ruin everything. It was for sure, certain, indubitable and indisputable that *absolutely nothing must go wrong tonight*. As well as Selina's, both his and Daisy's future depended upon tonight.

13

"Carlo is here," he said. "Shall we go down now?"

She gave him a radiant smile, then impulsively kissed his cheek. "Yes, I am ready. Oh, Uncle, I can't tell you how happy I am. I know I shall like Carlo's uncle and sister—Gemma is only two years younger than I, you know—and, from what Carlo says, they are quite prepared to like me. We shall all deal well together, I am sure."

"I am sure also," Flavian said, adding magnanimously, "How could they not like you?" He felt he could afford to let *some* of the elation he felt spill over as he took her arm and escorted her down the stairs.

Carlo, who was talking to Daisy—or rather, listening to Daisy talk—looked up just as Flavian and Selina reached the curve in the stairway, and the expression on his face was not lost on Flavian. As he had expected, the youth was speechless and his mouth stood agape in a most idiotish fashion.

"Good evening, Carlo," Selina said, apparently completely unaware of the effect she was causing. "Has it begun to snow yet?"

"N-no, not yet," he stammered, "but it is raw outside." Since both he and his sister had attended schools in England as children, his English was excellent and only in times of duress or extreme excitement did he resort to Italian, as he did now. *"Bellissima! Magnifica!"*

She smiled her thanks as he helped her with her cloak, and then the two of them were on their way. Flavian and Daisy stood at the window watching as they got into a carriage drawn by a handsome pair of matched grays, obviously lent to Carlo by his uncle for the evening since Carlo usually came calling in a gig drawn by a sorrel hardly larger than a pony.

"I shall be all a-tilt with nerves until she returns and tells us how it went," Daisy said, dropping the curtain and going back to hearthside.

"It will go quite well," Flavian prophesied, following his wife. "How should it go but well, with her being the most beautiful girl in all of England? Did you not see that sick-calf look on Carlo's face? Never have I seen anyone more in love! And the best part of it is that she has quite a *tendre* for him also, I think." He pinched his wife's arm playfully. "Daisy, me gel, from now on we'll all be living on the fat of the land instead of the lean. You mark my words, a new era is beginning for us."

With great solicitude Carlo spread the carriage robe across Selina's lap and then inquired as to whether she was warm enough. He seemed, Selina thought, a trifle nervous. He was more like a young man going to offer for his beloved than one taking his fiancée to meet a sister and uncle. This, of course, increased Selina's own nervousness which she had thought, until now, to be nonexistent.

"Are you afraid they will not like me?" she asked as the coachman cracked his whip over the grays as a signal to start.

Carlo laughed weakly. "What a silly notion!" he exclaimed. "There is no question about that. Gemma has already stated that you are to be her dearest friend as well as her sister."

"That will be nice," Selina said. "I have never had a sister nor, for that matter, a close friend of my own age."

"Neither has Gemma." Carlo laughed again, arousing Selina's suspicions further that the closer they came to Grosvenor Square, the more nervous he became.

"What about your uncle?" she asked. "Is he also pre-disposed to like me?"

"Oh, Aldo!" Carlo dismissed his uncle with a gesture as though what *he* thought was of little consequence. "One never knows what he thinks of anything or any-body—until he is ready to make his opinion known. Then he lets the whole world know."

"You mean he shouts?"

"No, only if he is excessively angry. He has other ways of letting everyone know what he thinks. One way is in his painting. If he decides he does not like a person, he will do a most unflattering drawing or portrait of him. Again, if he likes someone, the picture will be a masterpiece."

"You called him Aldo," she said. "Do you not call him Uncle Aldo?"

Again the strained laughter. "He is less than a dozen years older than I," he said, "and both Gemma and I feel that he is more of an older brother—except when he is angry at us. Then he is like a stern father."

It occurred to Selina that perhaps Carlo was worried for fear that Aldo would be like a stern father tonight rather than an older brother, but she did not pursue the conversation for Carlo had fallen silent and Selina thought it best to save further questions until the drive home when she was sure she would besiege him with literally dozens.

In addition to the happy excitement she felt, she also felt a sense of extreme contentment. She knew that for the past two years Flavin and Daisy—Flavian particularly—had wanted an advantageous marriage for her, but none of the men whom she had met socially measured up to what they wanted for her even though there had been one or two for whom she might have developed a *tendre* had she really put her mind to it. But Flavian had always said, "Wait a bit longer, me gel. After all, you are not in your caps yet and for one who looks like you, a better man will come along." Daisy had dashed ice water on his hopes, however, with the simple statement that "A better one will not come along to the places Selina goes. Do you expect her to meet a member of parliament at a party attended by clerks?"

Flavian had not answered, but a dark scowl had crossed his face. The next day he began moving heaven and earth to get a voucher to Almack's for Selina. But his efforts were to no avail for the Lady Patronesses considered themselves not only above earth, but also above heaven, and they could not be moved. Legend had it that once a royal princess even had difficulty getting into that famous marriage mart until her credentials were thoroughly checked. Selina had always doubted that particular story for she could never understand why a royal princess would *want* to get in Almack's.

After that, the parties Selina attended did not seem as pleasant to her for she realized that even if she met someone for whom she could feel the *grand passion*, she would not have the approval of Flavian and Daisy (certainly not Flavian, though Daisy might be coaxed into acquiescing) to marry the poor bloke (and that was undoubtedly what Flavian would call him).

Then Flavian had come home with an idea which had changed everything. He had been for a walk in the park and had noticed that much of the *haut ton* either went for walks or drives "obviously not for an outing, but to see and be seen." If Selina was to meet a "proper gentleman" it must be on *his* home turf, for he certainly was not coming to hers when he did not even know she existed. So Se-

17

lina began walking the paths in the park, sometimes alone, sometimes escorted by Flavian who also began taking her to concerts at Covent Garden, the theater in Drury Lane, and anywhere else that they could be a part of the *ton* without having their presence in that particular place questioned.

Flavian had been correct in his surmisings. As soon as the "proper gentlemen" took one look at Selina, they wanted to see more. And so they began to make her acquaintance . . . and then began the series of seemingly never-ending calls at the house in Half Moon Street. There was only one drawback: with so many to choose from, Selina could not settle on a single man, or even narrow the contestants to two or three. In time, she began to lose interest in all of them.

Then, during a solitary walk in the park on a warm summer afternoon, she had met Carlo; and Carlo, in turn, had met all the requirements demanded by Flavian, and what was more she even *liked* the shy young Italian (though, she confessed to him later, he had plied her with his attentions for several months before she realized she was genuinely fond of him and had come to think of him as more than just another of what Flavian referred to as her "string of beaux").

It was indeed fortunate for all concerned, she mused now, that her aunt and uncle-in-law had never insisted upon her marrying someone of *their* choice, for what would have followed would have made the war with Boney seem like a child's game with tin soldiers. Of an otherwise pleasant disposition, she had a streak of stubbornness which occasionally came to the fore and caused her either to wage battle or else to stand firm, whichever seemed called for, in the face of mountainous opposition.

That was a side of her Carlo had never seen, nor had Flavian and Daisy witnessed it more than once or twice. But Selina was very much aware that it was always lurking in the background, ready to appear when her defenses appeared to be down.

"Here we are." Carlo broke into her thoughts and she realized that the carriage had come to a halt in front of one of the largest of the Grosvenor Square mansions. "Just the three of you live here?" she blurted, amazed.

"Yes," Carlo said, helping her from the carriage. "Aldo said it was more house than he wanted, but it was the only one in this part of the city available at the time, and Aldo was determined to have it."

"He means to live here always?" she asked. Although Carlo had never told her so, she had it in the back of her mind that Aldo would someday, someday *soon*, go back to Italy while Carlo and his sister, who were educated in England, would remain in London.

But they were being greeted at the door by a butler in shining livery and there was no opportunity for Carlo to answer. "Mr. Barelli and Miss Gemma await you in the blue saloon," they were told.

Carlo took her arm, and she looked up at his finely chiseled face and smiled, but she was thinking: Oh, oh, the blue saloon! I hope it will not clash with my watergreen gown.

It did not. It was more like a backdrop on a stage which blended with whatever colors the actors wore. Selina's eyes took in first the entire room—as they had taken in the large, elegant entry hall—and then focused upon the people: first on Gemma because she was standing nearer. She was petite with long dark hair which curled over her shoulders. Her sparkling eyes, which seemed to hold concealed merriment, were as dark as her hair. To Selina she appeared more like a small, mischievous child than a young lady of eighteen years.

Without waiting for an introduction, Gemma came to her, both hands held out, and said, "Selina, you are even more beautiful than Carlo led us to believe, and he said you were the most beautiful girl in the world! I am so glad we are to be sisters."

"Thank you," Selina said, instantly liking the girl and her open friendliness. "I, too, am glad, and I have been looking forward to meeting you and . . ." She raised her eyes toward Aldo Barelli.

Her first thought was that she had never seen a more handsome man. He was very tall, with dark, curling hair like Gemma's, and perfect features and eyes that . . .

Her second thought was that there was something sinister about Aldo Barelli.

His eyes were dark like Carlo's and Gemma's but there was no merriment in them, concealed or otherwise. For that matter, she could not even detect welcome for her in them. Whatever the man was thinking was certainly not revealed in his eyes. There was, however, *something* in his eyes, something indefinable, something she would never be able to put into words if she wanted to describe him. Again, the word "sinister" came into her mind and she knew suddenly why Carlo had seemed nervous tonight for the first time.

"May I present my uncle, Aldo Barelli," Carlo said quickly, almost as though he had left the room and returned in the midst of a social crisis which only he could set aright.

"I am *very* pleased to meet you," Selina said, putting more enthusiasm into her words than she felt. Already the notion was well formed in her mind that she and Carlo's uncle would not deal well together.

Barelli made a formal bow, stared at Selina for a moment, a tiny flicker of a smile playing about his mouth (but definitely not reflected in his eyes) and said, "Shall we go in to dinner now?"

"So soon?" Gemma gasped. "But Aldo, I thought we were going to . . ."

"Yes, Aldo," Carlo interrupted, "I had a bottle of champagne brought up from the wine celler just for this occasion and I thought we . . ."

"They are ready to serve in the dining parlor, Carlo," Aldo said, "and you will find wine on the table, a good dry *Italian* wine and not this sickeningly sweet grape juice which the French foist on the world."

Selina looked from one to the other and decided that Aldo Barelli was one of the most thoroughly unpleasant people she had ever encountered.

"But we wanted to celebrate the engagement of Carlo and Selina," Gemma cried, the last words going up in a forlorn wail.

Aldo did not even bother to answer his niece but led the way to the dining parlor which was on the other side of the large entry hall. The room was a marvel of understated elegance, Selina thought, trying to take it all in without appearing to stare about her like a gawking ninnyhammer. The table in the center of the room was banquet length and was covered with the finest linen, and there were two matching candelabra in the center. The wall sconces also were silver and held long white tapers, and there were rose-colored hangings on the walls.

Aldo seated Gemma to the left of the head of the table

21

while Carlo seated Selina at the right and then sat down beside her. Aldo, of course, was at the head of the table.

Selina had a feeling there would not be much conversation during the meal (what in the whole wide world would she find to talk to the stern-looking, unfriendly man about?) and she was becoming more and more uncomfortable. But she was mistaken, for Gemma started in at once with a bright though inane line of chatter, and she tried to join in, thankful that the responses required little effort, for her thoughts were entirely with Carlo . . . and his uncle. Carlo occasionally glanced up at Aldo, an almost pleading look in his eyes which Selina could not begin to understand. If Aldo were opposed to the marriage, why had he agreed to invite her to dinner tonight? If he was not opposed, why was he acting so inhospitably toward her and so churlishly toward his niece and nephew? He not only did not contribute to the conversation, but he also did not even appear to be listening. Selina thought she had never seen such abominable rag-manners.

She could find no fault, however, with the food. It was both varied and excellently prepared, beginning with the soup, *verdure italiane*, and continuing with the crimped salmon, roast leg of lamb, green beans, mushroom fritters, potato cakes, several kinds of hot breads, and ending with *crème caramel*. It was all served by two footmen in livery, who seemed to anticipate Aldo's every wish. As they poured the dessert wine, Aldo raised his glass and, for the first time (although they had had wine with the other courses) proposed a toast. He looked at Selina, raised his glass higher, and said, "To your very good health—and happiness, Miss Bryand."

"Thank you," Selina murmured, wondering why she and Carlo had not been toasted simultaneously as was the

22

custom for engaged couples. But, giving him the benefit of the doubt, perhaps Aldo did not know that much about English customs . . . or manners. However, she reminded herself, Italians were *not* barbarians, and Aldo Barelli seemed to be very much *au courant* with English life in every other respect. After all, he had lived here for almost a year, and had apparently visited England many times before that.

As they were leaving the dining parlor, Aldo said to her, "Miss Bryand, have you ever seen any of my work?"

It was a minute before she realized he was referring to his paintings.

"No, I am sorry to say, I have not—unless you did the portraits in the blue saloon."

"No, they are family portraits which predate me by almost a century," he said. "Come, I will show you my studio. Gemma, Carlo, we shall have brandy and coffee in the bookroom. You may wait for us there."

It had not been a suggestion he gave them but an order. Carlo looked at Selina regretfully as Aldo took her arm and escorted her up the winding stairs to the second story and then to the third.

He lit three lamps in the small room into which he ushered her, saying, "Of course, seeing the paintings at night, you will get only a general idea of the work. By daylight you could view them more critically."

She could not help but wonder how well he would take criticism. He did not strike her as being a person one could criticize easily—at least not without fear of dreadful consequences. However, as she looked at the painting on the easel nearest the door, she not only could not imagine anyone's daring to criticize him, but she also could not conceive of anyone's *wanting* to. It was a painting of a

23

woman, a young woman whose beauty was perfection. She had cascading dark hair, big brown eyes which looked so alive that Selina had the eerie sensation that the woman was staring back at her, asking her some question. There was also a haunting quality about the lovely face in the portrait. Selina looked at it for a long time without speaking. Then she said, "She is lovely and the painting itself, though I am not an artist nor a qualified judge of art, seems quite remarkable to me. Is she . . . was she your wife?"

"I am unmarried," her host said, obviously pleased by her reaction to his work. "She was my sister, the mother of Carlo and Gemma."

Selina looked at the portrait again, even more interested now. "Is this something you have done recently?" she asked.

"Yes, it is just completed. I did it from memory since we have no likenesses of Jacinth. She died six years ago at the age of thirty-four. She is somewhat younger in the painting, you will notice, because that is the way I remember her. Now . . . let us go quickly to some of the other paintings."

Selina was unsure whether he was rushing her along because memories of his dead sister were painful or because he was in a hurry to have done with this one civility he had shown since she came into the house.

She glanced around the room for the first time and saw that it was almost full of paintings—easels everywhere, and some paintings on the floor along the walls. There was a round skylight above which appeared to be a tremendous night-black eye overlooking the room. She felt a sudden chill as she looked up, and she shuddered visibly.

"It is too cold for you here," Aldo said immediately, "so we shall look at no more."

"Oh, no," she said quickly, "I do honestly want to see the others, for I am quite impressed."

He acknowledged this compliment with a nod of his head as though accepting what was due him. "Actually, Miss Bryand, I did not bring you here to show you my work. I have something I want to say to you." He paused, then added, "So I shall say it quickly and we can return to the others."

His face had taken on a dark, serious look which was as frightening as the momentary glance up at the black skylight had been. Selina could think of nothing to say. She simply stood looking at him, unable even to imagine what to expect.

"I asked Carlo not to bring you here tonight," Aldo said without preamble, "but he insisted. He said if I saw you, I would change my mind—but it is not a case of changing *my* mind. The fact is, we cannot change fate, can we? We cannot change what is to be."

"I have not the least notion what you are talking about," Selina said spiritedly, suddenly becoming a bit miffed with her host who in a trice seemed to have reverted to his earlier inhospitable manner.

"You and Carlo cannot be married. Not now, not at any time in the future. No, wait, let me finish, then you may say whatever you wish. I know of no other way to tell you except just to come right out with it. Believe me, I wish I could lessen the blow . . ."

"What *are* you talking about?" Selina interrupted. "You are making no sense whatever."

"Carlo cannot marry you," he repeated. "He already is

engaged, and has been for a number of years, to a young lady in Italy."

Selina gave a mirthless half-laugh. "You will have to think of a better reason than that, Mr. Barelli. Carlo is twenty now—the same age as I—and I doubt if he has been engaged to *any*one for several years. Who would take seriously an offer of marriage from a mere *boy?*"

"My dear Miss Bryand, is it possible that you do not realize that marriages are *arranged* sometimes even for babes before they have left their cradles? It happens quite often in Italy—and I'm sure is not unknown here in England."

Selina hesitated before replying. If it were true that a marriage had been arranged between Carlo and someone else, why had he not told her? Could it be because he no longer considered that arrangement binding? Of course, that had to be the answer! Carlo had fallen in love with her the moment he first saw her (he had told her that often enough), and whatever plans had been made for his future had been put aside by him at that moment.

"It is not unheard of, Mr. Barelli," she answered finally, "in Italy as well as here, for an engagement to be broken. Now that Carlo is old enough to decide for himself whom he wants to marry, I do not think he would let an arrangement made by someone else in his behalf stand in his way."

Aldo Barelli shook his head slowly. "I was afraid I would not be able to make you understand, Miss Bryand, but for Carlo's sake I wanted to try. You see, after Carlo's father—and my friend—Pasquale Moraldo died, it was not long before the family became very short of funds, so my sister was forced to sell the Moraldo family estate. At that time, Carlo was twelve or thirteen. The people who bought the property had a daughter only a year younger and they—having taken a great fancy to Carlo—said that if, when Carlo became twenty-one, he would marry their daughter, Maria, his family home would be given back to him as a wedding gift."

He paused and waited, but Selina was incapable of speech.

"It is not the cold, mercenary arrangement you might think," Aldo continued. "Carlo and Maria became great friends after my sister Jacinth brought him and Gemma to live with me. You see, my property bordered on the Moraldo property so the youngsters saw much of each other as they were growing up. Then, some years ago, I proposed sending Carlo and Gemma to England to school. I wanted them to have more or less the same education that I had had, and I came here to school as a boy. Carlo continued to see Maria on vacations, however, and—until he met you—their plans were firm and unchangeable. This time the wedding plans were made *by* them and not *for* them. They are to be married on Carlo's twenty-first birthday, and that, as you know, is only three months away."

He paused again, then went on when she said nothing. "Within the next week or so, Carlo is to go back to Italy to begin preparations for the wedding and for taking over the Moraldo property."

"And what has Carlo to say about that?" She finally managed to get the words out.

"Carlo at first pleaded with me to go back to Italy for him and extricate him from the whole affair. I told him if his father's ancestral home meant no more to him than

27

that, he should at least think of his sister. Although I am happy to provide for Gemma, I think eventually she would be happier in her own country, and I have made plans to remain in England. Also, Carlo has only what I give to him and, although I am far from being a poor man, I think it would be a burden to his pride to have me take on *his* family to support."

"You said Carlo *at first* pleaded with you. What does he say now?" she asked.

"He thought that by bringing you here tonight, he could get me to change my mind. I must tell you, Miss Bryand, that there is no possibility of that. To me it is a matter of honor as well as Carlo's duty to return to Italy, marry Maria, and take his rightful place as master of the house and manager of the Moraldo villa. Against my better judgment, I humored him by letting you come tonight." He looked straight into her eyes but, as before, she could not tell what he was thinking. "When he returns from taking you home, I shall tell him that he will leave for Italy within a fortnight," he said.

"And if he refuses to go?"

"You apparently do not know him very well, Miss Bryand. He will not refuse."

Again, Selina stood in stunned silence, her mind going over everything Aldo Barelli had said. For some reason, she began to have a deep feeling of humiliation, as though she had been brought to this house for the sole purpose of being insulted. Why had Carlo not told her any of this before instead of allowing the glowering Aldo to do it for him? Was Carlo that much a coward? For a moment, she did not know whom she despised more, Carlo or his uncle.

Without a word, she walked out of the room and started down the stairs, aware that Aldo was right behind her.

"I am sorry," he said with something like a note of gentleness in his voice for the first time. "I did not want to have to tell you this."

She went down both flights of stairs without answering him. Then, at the bottom, she turned around and faced him. "Will you make my excuses to Carlo and Gemma? I am going now."

"Carlo will want to see you safely home," Aldo said. "I will get him . . ."

"No!" she almost screamed. "I would rather not see him again." In truth, she did not trust herself to see him again. She was afraid that if she did she would burst into tears, losing the control she was trying so hard to maintain.

"Then I shall see you home myself," he said.

"No!" she cried again. "If you will just tell your coachman that I am ready to go, I would appreciate it. I do not need to be escorted. Please understand, Mr. Barelli, that I do not wish to see you again either."

Holding herself stiffly erect, she motioned for the butler to get her wrap, and turned her back on Aldo as the butler helped her with the cloak. Without looking at her host again, she marched to the door and then outside to wait for the carriage to be brought around.

It was only when she was in the carriage on her way home that it occurred to her that she had neither wished her host a good-night nor thanked him for his hospitality.

Hospitality?

Her marvelous control left her then and she began to

29

cry into her hands, fervently wishing that the carriage would never reach Half Moon Street so she would not have to tell Flavian and Daisy about the terrible thing that had happened.

Two

Flavian stirred up the fire, emitted a long sigh, and resumed his seat in the chair opposite Daisy's. "I fear this is going to be an unusually long evening," he said.

"Yes," she agreed, "but have patience. You, especially, have been looking forward to this for a long time."

"Two years," he said. "Ever since I knew we would be taking Selina in with us. It isn't that I'm not fond of the girl, Daisy," he hastened to add, "you know that I am. But from the moment I first laid eyes on her I predicted a fortune could be made by an advantageous marriage for her although, at the time, I wasn't aware that it would be *our* fortune as well as hers. And now—"

"Now it will soon come about," Daisy finished for him. "Everything has worked out beautifully for all of us."

Flavian leaned back in his chair and closed his eyes. He sighed again, but this time in contentment. Soon he would be well taken care of by Carlo Moraldo (or whoever held the purse strings in the family) and he could take his ease until the end of time. For the rest of his life, he could live the way he had always wanted to, with a valet, a butler, a cook, footmen, and enough maid-servants to see that Daisy never had to lift a finger. No more pretense about the servants not being there because of illness, no more pretense about anything. From the day Selina became Mrs. Carlo Moraldo, life for all of them would be as easy as sliding down a greased Maypole.

And, best of all, he would never have to go into another gaming-hell for the purpose of keeping body and soul together.

Flavian knew that he had been born into this world as a mass of contradictions rather than as a normal baby boy. For as long as he could remember, he had had an all-consuming, driving ambition to better himself and his station in life, and that ambition had been offset by an innate laziness, an indolence that was as incapacitating as a terminal disease. They balanced each other perfectly on his inner scale: aspiration and sloth. And what did he do about it? Naturally, nothing. Occasionally the ambition would lead him to make plans for a course of action, and then the plans would be canceled out by the indolence. Born the son of a smithy (a trade he both loathed and looked down upon), in a tiny village near London, he knew that by the time he reached his majority—as did his family know—that he would never amount to a row of pins. The difference in their thinking, however, was that while his family despaired, he realized that without exerting too much effort he could survive by his wits. He knew he had a good mind and he did not object to using it as long as he did not have to use it too often. He wanted wealth and all its accouterments and trappings.

The best way to attain it, he decided, was to marry it. He was a good-looking young man and quite presentable for he was an avid observer of the ways of the gentility and he adopted those ways as his own with no difficulty. Unfortunately, before he met a young lady with all the necessary qualifications, he met Daisy and fell top-over-tail in love with her. Though no great beauty, she was attractive in a little-girl sort of way which brought out an unsuspected protective instinct in him. Nothing would do but he must marry her. So marry her he did, and at the same time said fare-thee-well to his dreams of marrying into enormous wealth. Although Daisy's family was in better circumstances than his own, the difference was not that great.

How did he take care of his young wife? From time to time—before starvation became imminent—he would go to the forge with his father and work for a few days. And he would win at cards.

He was not a gambler by nature, but he discovered shortly after his seventeenth birthday that he possessed an uncanny skill at every card game he tried. He was so good that his friends and neighbors stopped playing with him (on the advice of wives and mothers who were wont to say, "You might as well throw your money down a rat-hole; you will lose it just as surely if you gamble at cards with Flavian Curtis").

Lack of players caused Flavian to venture into the gaming-houses of London and he found, somewhat to his surprise, that his amazing luck held out there also. He was never known to lose at cards. However, he was not so lucky at other forms of gambling. At the tables, he lost. At the wheels, he lost. And at Newmarket, he lost everything. He told himself that as the son of a smithy he

33

should have known that the hated horses would be unlucky for him.

Se he stuck with cards—when it was necessary. The strange thing was that he really did not enjoy playing cards for money, for it made the game too strenuous, too nerve-tautening. He would much rather have played just for the sheer enjoyment of it and money be damned.

He and Daisy had been married for nearly two years when he decided that the thing to do was to move to London. Actually, he had decided long before, but it took time to convince Daisy who did not want to move further away from her family. After two days of cards in several different gaming houses (he never liked to win too much in one place; it made other gamblers leery of him), he had enough money to buy the house in Bulton Street— and that was where they still lived years later when Daisy's niece, Selina, let them know that she was completely without funds and had nowhere to go and needed a home. Flavian, instead of being opposed to her coming to them, looked upon her arrival as "Fate's plan for Daisy and me." He had seen Selina at her mother's funeral and had commented on her extraordinary beauty. Such beauty could not fail to attract a man of title and wealth and, he reasoned, since he an Daisy would share their all with Selina, she would later share with them.

But there was one thing that he knew beyond the shadow of a doubt: wealth attracts wealth. Unless Selina had at least the *appearance* of wealth, no man of means would so much as glance her way. Bulton Street was decidedly not the place for the three of them to live.

Before Selina arrived, Flavian made a trip to Paris. He knew it would take much more money than he had ever won before and he did not want to take it from any man who might be a prospective husband for Selina, so he left London. Who would marry a girl whose guardian was a professional gambler? In two weeks he had amassed enough to pay for the trip and to buy the house in Half Moon Street—which he and Daisy moved into only days before Selina arrived.

He could, he supposed, win enough to have the servants he wanted, but somehow it did not seem worth the effort. It would mean that he would have to sit at cards two or three times a week, and that was too much like work.

Everything has worked out beautifully for all of us. He mentally echoed Daisy's words as he waited for the front door to open and Selina to rush in, rapturous over her conquest of Carlo's family. But it would be at least another hour, possibly two, before the girl and her happy, love-struck fiance returned.

He looked over at Daisy. "I would be willing to wager a monkey that you already have the wedding planned, down to the last small detail."

She grinned sheepishly and nodded. "I thought you were not a betting man."

"I'm not. Merely a figure of speech. Gambling is not . . ."

Whatever he was about to say that gambling was not was left hanging in mid-air, for at that moment the front door opened and a shivering, downcast Selina came in.

Flavian stood up. "Where is Carlo? I thought he would come in with you. I have a bottle of champagne . . ." He stopped, noticing the expression on Selina's face.

Daisy already had taken in the dejected look, the slight stoop of the shoulders and the quivering lower lip. She rushed to Selina, saying "What *is* it, dear? Surely you

35

are not going to say Carlo's uncle and sister did not like you! I would never believe it."

Selina cast off her cloak. "It doesn't signify whether they like me or not. Carlo cannot marry me because he is going to marry someone else, a girl in Italy. He is going back there to live."

There was a silence of about two minutes while Flavian and Daisy both stared at her unbelievingly. Then Flavian began shaking his head and saying over and over, "That is not true. It simply is *not* true. You are telling us a Banbury tale."

Selina, who though visibly shaken had remained in control, now began to cry silently. For a minute or two the tears slid down her cheeks unrestrained, and then, as though willing herself to numbness, she stopped crying and in a monotone related to them the events of the evening.

She had hardly finished her story when Flavian cried, "Why that foreign, good-for-nothing, lying, young whippersnapper! We will sue him, that's what we'll do! I'll have him haled into court for breach of promise. We will show him that he can't . . ."

"No!" Selina and Daisy cried simultaneously.

"We will do no such thing," Selina went on. "I—I could not stand the embarrassment of it."

"Embarrassment be damned!" Flavian shouted. "He did offer for you, did he not?"

"You know that he did," Selina said. "I understand he spoke to you before he did to me. All very proper."

"And you accepted the offer, did you not?" Flavian appeared to hear no voice but his own.

"Yes, I did," Selina said very softly.

"Then that is as clear a case of breach of promise as

36

any I have ever heard." Flavian rubbed his hands together in satisfaction. "He is going to pay and pay well for trifling with your affections."

"No," Selina said again. "It would be mortifying for me."

"And just what *do* you intend doing about it, if I may make bold to ask?' His anger appeared to be directed toward Selina now as much as toward the alleged wrongdoer.

"Nothing."

"Nothing!"

"Nothing at all."

"You have taken leave of your senses, and that is the God's truth."

Daisy spoke for the first time in a long while. "The truth is, Selina is right. If we took this matter to court there would be all kinds of talk and notoriety, and it would not be favorable to Selina—it never is to the woman, no matter how innocent a victim she may be. Men would exchange sly winks and say . . . all sorts of things."

For once, Flavian had no ready answer.

In a softer tone, Daisy continued, "It might ruin her chances of . . . of ever making a suitable match."

Flavian nodded, still silent. He could see the logic of this and was glad Daisy had stopped him from making a foolish mistake.

Selina, who had been watching the two of them and listening to the exchange as though they were talking about someone she hardly knew, turned suddenly and headed for the stairs.

"Where are you going?" Flavian asked. "Wait, we haven't settled anything yet."

Selina gave him a long, hard look and said, "It was settled when I walked out of that house. I never want to see or hear from any of them again." With that, she went upstairs.

"I have never seen her so bitter before," Daisy commented.

"She has never before had so much to be bitter about," Flavian said. "Dash it all to hell, what are we going to do now?" He sat down again and buried his face in his hands, then looked up and said, "I thought we had everything settled—her future and ours. And now—now we have to start planning all over again. Oh!" he groaned.

"She is only twenty," Daisy said. "It isn't as though she were thirty, or even five and twenty."

"Most girls are already married—some long married—by the time they are twenty. And now . . ." He stopped when a thought occurred to him suddenly. He had never felt so depressed.

"What is it, Flavian?" Daisy asked.

"It isn't going to happen again," he said disconsolately. "We are not going to find another man like Carlo for her because . . ."

"We didn't find Carlo," Daisy interrupted, "Selina did."

"You know what I mean. Carlo is a young, impulsive, very-much-in-love Italian. Englishmen, even top-over-tail in love Englishmen, are inclined to be a bit more practical and not so impulsive. An Englishman will want to know about the size of her dowry—that is, anyone we would consider a suitable match would want to know. And if *he* didn't, his family would. It is hopeless. Hopeless!"

"You didn't consider it hopeless before she met Carlo, so why should it be any more hopeless now?" Daisy asked practically.

"I was beginning to consider it hopeless then, only I didn't tell you for fear of depressing you."

"It isn't as though it is impossible to find a husband for her."

"I *know* that," he said irritably. "If we did not care a whit whom or what she married, they would be lined up at the door waiting to offer for her, just as they used to be." His face was the picture of dejection. "No, Daisy, me gel, it's no use—we might as well admit it. Selina will never marry a title or, for that matter, a man of wealth or vast property holdings."

Daisy was quiet, mulling over this bit of enlightened speculation. "I suppose you are right," she said finally.

"I know I am right," he said. "And with her beauty, what a waste! The only way it would stand her in good stead would be if she were not too particular about the morality of it and had aspirations of becoming a rich man's mistress . . ."

He broke off suddenly and looked across at Daisy. His expression was somewhat like sunrise: a little light, a small smile, gradually increasing until the radiance was almost blinding. He jumped up, snapped his fingers and said, "That's it!"

Daisy looked at him questioningly.

"There isn't a man in England or on the Continent who would not be happy to set Selina up as his mistress."

"She would never consent to such a thing." Daisy motioned the idea away as though it were a small, annoying fly. "You know Selina well enough to know that she would never agree to anything like that."

"If the man were rich enough, great enough, it would make all the difference," Flavian said. "Just look back

39

through history and you will find the women almost as famous as the men they . . ."

"Infamous, you mean," Daisy interrupted. "And just where do you propose she meet these men who are going to be so enthralled with the sight of her that they will rush to give her not only everything *her* heart desires but *your* heart's desires as well?"

"What's wrong with Carlton House? After all, that is where the *crème de la crème* is to be found these days—and nights."

"Flavian Curtis, you are all about in your head! Dear heaven above us, you couldn't get her in Almack's and now you are talking about getting her into one of Prinny's gatherings! Next, you will be talking about getting her into Prinny's *bed*!"

Flavian chortled and suddenly began to dance a little jig. He leaned over Daisy and kissed the tip of her nose. "Daisy, me gel, what would I do without you? That's exactly the thing. The whole world knows what a lover of beauty is our Prince Regent. He will think Selina a treasure beyond compare, and she will be as adored by him as Nell Gwyn was by Charles the Second." He kissed Daisy again, this time on the cheek. "That is exactly the thing! Selina will be a mistress to the Regent."

Three

Selina awoke the following morining with a heaviness that was almost tangible. Her first thought was: Something terrible has happened, but what? It was exactly the way she had felt on awakening the morning after her parents had been killed, the day the pattern of her life began to change. It was a sensation she had expected never to experience again, but here it was, that burning oppressive heaviness, holding her down like molten lead.

Then, as unwanted consciousness overcame drowsiness, she remembered the night before and its disastrous events. She realized that her life was out of control again, once more being changed drastically. Her plans for a pleasurable and loving future with Carlo had been put aside (Flavian would say by Fate) as easily as though they had never existed in the first place. And Carlo, whom she had thought she knew well, understood well, and loved well, apparently was a weakling who was going to do nothing to prevent his and her plans from being discarded like so much unwanted refuse.

However, while she thought little of Carlo now, she thought even less of his uncle for making Carlo go through with a marriage which he did not want to a girl for whom he had no love. Carlo loved *her*, not some girl in Italy whom he had seen only occasionally in the past few years. Why did he not stand up to his uncle and say, "I love Selina and I shall never marry anyone but her."

Back to her original thought: he did not do so because he was weak. It was easier for him to have his whole life arranged; it was more pleasant and comfortable not to go against the wishes of Aldo Barelli.

Then she remembered Barelli's words: It is not the cold, mercenary arrangement you might think. Carlo and Maria became great friends . . . they saw much of each other growing up . . . until he met you their plans were firm and unchangeable . . . this time the wedding plans were made by them and not for them.

He had been happy with his Maria before he met Selina and he would be happy with her again after they were reunited in Italy. Selina had no doubt now that he would go back home and forget all about his love in London as soon as he and Maria were together again. The wedding would be held, as scheduled, on his twenty-first birthday.

She sat up in bed, trying to blot out the image of Carlo and Maria together, happily sharing the rest of their lives at Villa Moraldo.

I could have been the one, she thought, had it not been for Aldo Barelli. He is to blame for the ruin my life is in.

She got out of bed and began to dress, choosing a French cambric of somber gray, totally in keeping with

42

her mood. What would become of her now? What would she do with the rest of her life which seemed to stretch so endlessly before her? She was, like Wordsworth, having intimations of immortality and what she really wanted was mortality, and that right soon.

It was very clear to her that she would never be blessed with a marriage for love and so (for Daisy's and Flavian's sake as well as her own) she had better settle for a marriage of convenience . . . and that right soon also. But she most assuredly would make it *her* convenience. Never again would she be vulnerable; never again would she be hurt.

Her toilette completed, she went downstairs to the breakfast parlor to find Daisy and Flavian already finished with breakfast, but still lingering over coffee.

"Good morning, dear," Daisy spoke first. "I do hope you managed to get a good night's rest in spite of . . ."

"Now, Daisy," Flavian interrupted, "we will not speak of that unpleasant episode again. You just forget it, Selina. Let it go out of your mind as though it never happened."

Selina nodded, managing a weak smile. Flavian was proposing the impossible, of course, but that was not unusual for him. Many of his ideas were just as farfetched, and some of them were so farfetched that they actually worked. That was what she had to remember: it might, someday, be possible to forget she had ever heard of Carlo Moraldo . . . and Aldo Barelli.

"I will get your breakfast," Daisy said, getting up from the table.

"No, don't bother," Selina said quickly. "I am really not very hungry. Just coffee will do."

"No, you need more. You must keep your strength

43

up." Daisy went toward the door, looking back over her shoulder and shaking her head at Flavian as though reminding him of something he was or was not supposed to do. Probably, Selina thought, something he was not supposed to say. She wondered briefly what it was, then promptly forgot it as she sipped the hot coffee she had just poured and felt it burn all the way to her stomach.

"Anything you need?" Flavian asked. "I have to go out to market for Daisy."

"Nothing, thank you." Nothing except Carlo, nothing except for last night never to have happened.

Flavian got up, came around the table to her and kissed her forehead. "I said we wouldn't talk about it anymore, and we won't, but I just want to say this. You shouldn't worry, because you are well rid of that spineless, sniveling, unprincipled wretch. For your sake—and Daisy's—I will not call him out, but if I ever happen to run into him anywhere, I shall . . ."

"No, Uncle, you must not feel that way," she said quickly. "I want your promise that you and Carlo will never come to blows—and as for talking about this . . . this contretemps in the future, if it should come up in conversation naturally, I will not mind, not too much anyway."

Grumblingly, Flavian gave her the promise she asked and left, still muttering under his breath about the spineless, sniveling, unprincipled wretch.

Daisy returned bearing a plate of eggs, ham and muffins. Selina stared in horror. "Surely you do not expect me to eat all that," she said.

"Eat what you want," Daisy said. "Sometimes you can get solace from food, or so I have heard." She had never known how to show her feelings and that included

44

showing sympathy or emotion over another's trouble, and so she was trying, in the only way she knew, to let Selina know she cared.

Realizing this, Selina ate . . . and ate . . . and ate, which was her way of letting Daisy know that she understood and was grateful.

Just as she was finishing the mammoth breakfast, she heard the knocker on the outside door and started to answer, but Daisy got up first, saying, "I will go." She returned almost immediately, her face white, and said, "It is Carlo. He wants to see you."

"You may tell him that I do not want to see him. I made that clear to his uncle last night." Fury was taking possession of her at the gall of the spineless, sniveling, unprincipled wretch, but then a thought occurred to her: Perhaps Aldo Barelli had not delivered her message to Carlo. "Wait," she said as Daisy was about to leave the room. "Show him into the drawing room. I will see him."

"Are you sure . . ." Daisy began.

"I will see him this one time, then never again," Selina said.

She purposely sipped the remaining coffee slowly, wanting to keep him waiting, wanting to increase his apprehension (if he had any), wanting to have him at a decided disadvantage. She thought again of the vow she had made to herself before she had gotten out of bed: she would never allow anyone to hurt her again. She most certainly would not allow the same man to hurt her twice.

Slowly, in complete control, she went to the drawing room, her posture rigidly stiff, her manner cold enough to have iced over the English Channel.

Daisy, after ushering Carlo into the drawing room, had disappeared into another part of the house. When Selina went into the room, Carlo was standing beside the blue velvet chair, nervously making strange patterns by running his fingers against the grain of the velvet. Seeing Selina, he went to her at once.

"My dearest, I did not expect you to leave last night before I could explain . . ."

"There was no reason to stay," Selina said coldly. "Mr. Barelli did a quite adequate job of explaining everything."

"I did not even know he planned to tell you . . ."

"There seems to be quite a lot that you do not know, Carlo."

He tried to take her hand but she pulled away from him as though he were a rabid dog.

"Please, Selina . . . please just listen to me for a minute. I am not sure what Aldo said to you. He probably told you about Maria . . . and all that. I *am* sure he did not tell you that none of that matters to me now . . . indeed, it has not mattered since I first saw you. You are my love, my only love . . ."

"Carlo," she said, weariness in her voice, "I am finding this all very tiresome."

He appeared startled at this response. "But . . . but . . ."

"You are a coward," she declared, "and as for your uncle, I can say unqualifiedly that he has the most abominable rag-manners it has ever been my misfortune to witness. Now, if you will excuse me . . ."

"Selina, we are *engaged* to be married. Have you forgotten *that*? You have not called off the engagement, nor have I, and so we are still officially engaged. What I came here to tell you . . . to ask you, rather . . ."

"You may consider the engagement broken," Selina interrupted. "As of this moment, I am calling it off. If it were possible to call it off retroactively, I would."

". . . to ask you . . . Selina, let us go away together at once and be married. We could go to Gretna Green, anywhere . . . Aldo need not know about it until it is a *fait accompli*, and then he will accept it . . . I know he will . . . and say no more about my going back to Italy and marrying Maria." He talked so fast that the words seemed to tumble over each other. "Aldo will relent eventually . . . he is sure to . . . and until then we can live on your dowry. It will be no time at all until I am back in his good graces again, and then everything will be just as we planned it from the beginning. Aldo liked you, I am sure of it . . . I could tell even though he did not have much to say last night . . . Please, Selina, please say we can still be married. Let's just forget that last night ever happened, shall we?"

Selina stared at him as though he were a recent escapee from Bedlam. "You and your mind either have parted company or else you are still a dim-witted child." She said it, not with malice, but as though making a discovery about him.

"It will take him a week only, perhaps a fortnight, to change his mind," Carlo went on, ignoring all insults. "As I said, we can live on your dowry until . . ."

Her laughter interrupted him. It was almost with pleasure that she said, "I have no dowry, Carlo. I thought you knew that I haven't a feather to fly with and neither do my aunt and uncle."

He stared at her in amazement, his mouth hanging open.

"Did you not catch on to that fact by the way my uncle kept referring to the ailing servants. Surely in all the time you have been coming here you must have realized that we have no servants, never have had any. This house was

47

left to my uncle by a relative he never even knew, otherwise we would be living in one of those poor little houses on Bulton Street."

Carlo, outraged, found his voice. "How can you insinuate that you were deceived and treated unfairly knowing that you were doing just that to me from the moment we met? Aldo was right all along; you and I were never meant to marry."

These words only added to Selina's fury at Aldo Barelli. "I never told you I had a dowry or that my relatives were well-off," she snapped.

"Well, you implied . . ."

"I have implied nothing. That is not my way!"

"I am leaving." Carlo turned and stalked toward the door, acting as though his departure was the ultimate tragedy in the life of any girl.

"The pity is that you ever came at all," Selina said.

At the door he turned and gave her one quick, sad glance and then he left the house.

Numb and unblinking, Selina listened for the sound of horse hooves as the gig moved down Half Moon Street, taking Carlo Moraldo out of her life forever. She was standing beside the same blue velvet chair where Carlo had stood when she entered the room and, unconsciously, her finger was tracing the same strange pattern his had made as he rubbed against the grain of the velvet.

Four

When Flavian returned from marketing, he found Selina sitting trance-like in the drawing room. He went straight to the pantry, relieved himself of his bundles, then found Daisy in the cook-room.

"Is she ill?" were his first words.

"She had a visitor right after you went out," Daisy said. "Carlo came."

"Did they . . ."

"Nothing is changed," Daisy said.

"That unprincipled, dastardly . . ."

"Calling him names is not going to help anything."

"It helps me!" Flavian declared. "And it would help me even more if I were to call him out."

"Help you into an early grave," Daisy said, alarmed for fear he might try to do just that. No matter what weapons were chosen, Carlo, because of his age, would have a decided advantage.

49

"She is sitting in there looking like death itself," Flavian said.

"Stunned," Daisy said, "but her age is an advantage for her, also. She will recover, even though she may not think so right now."

"I was just thinking," Flavian said slowly, "this may be the right time to break the news to her . . . that is, to tell her what we have decided . . ."

"What *you* have decided," Daisy amended.

". . . will be best for her future," Flavian went on. "Since she is already in something of a state of shock, this news will not be a stunner for her."

"I would not count on that," Daisy said, "but I agree that if you are going to tell her at all, you may as well tell her now and get it done with."

Flavian took a deep breath, gave Daisy a look which she could not decipher and went into the drawing room. Selina hardly even glanced up as he entered.

"Selina, me gel, I think we should have a little talk," he said.

"Yes, I know, Uncle." Her voice sounded as though she were bone-tired and speaking to him from a long and wearying distance. "I know both you and Aunt are as unhappy as I about the outcome of my . . . my . . . Well, I came to a decision this morning. I shall do what I can to replace Carlo as soon as possible. I shall marry . . ."

"Selina, your aunt and I have been talking about it," he interrupted, "and we are not sure it is in your best interests to think about marriage . . . at least, not right now." He had a slight feeling of guilt at including Daisy in the conniving, but not enough to make him omit her name as one of the sculptors of The Plan.

Selina looked up at him with sudden interest in her

eyes. "Yes, Uncle? I should be curious to know what you think *is* in my best interests right now."

He had no idea how to break his indelicate idea to her delicately. "I, er . . . that is, *we* think that you would be far, far better off as . . . as the mistress to a wealthy and famous man."

She looked at him, disbelief clear in her large brown eyes. Then she managed a smile and said, "I would hardly have thought of jesting at a time like this, but . . ."

"I am not jesting," Flavian said stoutly. "I—we—talked it all over last night after you retired, the advantages and the disadvantages, and quite frankly, we could not think of any disadvantages." He held up his hand as she was about to speak. "Think back through history, Selina. The mistresses of men of consequence have been well-remembered, *important* women. Important in their *own* right. There was Nero's Poppaea Sabina, much cherished by Nero and . . ."

"As I remember, she died as the result of a kick from Nero." Selina stated the historical fact tonelessly.

Startled, but not deterred by this bit of information, Flavian went on, "And there was the Marquise de Pompadour who was not only the mistress of Louis the Fifteenth but also controlled him completely, as well as the whole political situation in France."

"And she caused the Seven Years' War which was disastrous to France," Selina rebutted.

Still undaunted, Flavian continued, "And in our own country there was Nell Gwyn, mistress of Charles the Second whose affection she held until his death. She even bore him two sons, one of whom became a duke. She neither started a war nor came to a tragic end. You know why she fared better than the other two? I will tell you."

51

The idea had come to him suddenly. "Because the English are more civilized about these things than the French and the Italians. After all, Nero was a barbarian and as for Louis the Fifteenth . . ."

"Uncle, this seems to me like a lot of useless conversation unless you are leading up to something definite which you want to say. If so, please get on with it."

He looked her straight in the eyes and said, "There is no reason on God's green earth why you should not be a mistress to our Prince Regent."

She stared at him, speechless, her eyes becoming rounder and rounder, and then she burst into peals of helpless laughter. Finally, controlling her mirth, she said, "You are doing a remarkably good job of cheering me up, Uncle, and I thank you. I cannot think of anything more ludicrous than me with the lecherous Prinny."

It had not occurred to him that she would think he was jesting. "I am serious, Selina," he said, "*very* serious. And I do not think you should malign our monarch."

This caused Selina to go into more gales of laughter. "Not malign him!" she gasped, trying to get her breath. "I wish I could remember all the names I have heard you call him. Let me see . . . wastrel, womanizer, unconscionable scoundrel. Those are only a few. Surely you cannot expect me to take seriously such a tottyheaded idea."

In the sternest tones, Flavian said, "I—that is, your aunt and I—think it would be most advantageous for you, even more so than marriage, if you were to become the Regent's mistress. Now, I don't know how I can say it more plainly or more seriously than that."

"Dear God, I believe you mean it!" Her astonishment was so great that she could hardly get the words out.

"I never meant anything more."

"You want me to . . . Uncle, you have gone insane! In the first place, even if I *wanted* to become . . . that scourge's mistress, there isn't the slightest chance that I could even *meet* him."

"You let me take care of that," Flavian said. "Have you not heard of our Regent's love for beautiful things? And you, me gel, are beautiful indeed. He will treasure you as woman has never been treasured before. You will be . . ."

"I will be nothing," she interrupted. "I have not the slightest desire even to be in the same room with that reptile. Have you not heard that he is referred to as the Prince of Pleasure, among other apt epithets. And the Duke of Wellington called him and his brothers 'the damn'dest millstones about the neck of any government that can be imagined.'"

"What he lacks in political knowledge he more than makes up in other ways," Flavian said. "Why, he has set a whole new style of dress, and look what he has done for the architecture of this once drab old city. He has made elegant living, once something to be despised as evil, both acceptable and desirable. He has spared no expense in beautifying Carlton House, Buckingham Palace, the castle at Windsor, and in collecting some of the finest paintings, china, furniture, jewelry and works of art in the world. He will be remembered for . . ."

". . . for bankrupting the country," Selina finished, "for causing his poor subjects to suffer all kinds of deprivation because of his idiotish openhanded spending. And as for treasuring a mistress, dear Uncle, I would not say—if the past is any indication—that he has treasured *any*one, wife or mistress. Take Mrs. Fitzherbert . . ."

"My dear gel, he *married* her, didn't he?"

53

"And then disclaimed the ceremony, saying it was not legal. The whole of England was shocked, and his father, the King, was so furious that . . ."

"Oh, come, Selina," Flavian interjected. "After all, the King picked out a royal princess for George to marry."

Selina all but snorted in a most unladylike way. "What a sad, shabby time of it Princess Caroline had. She admitted publicly that her husband was drunk on their wedding night, extremely rude to her at all times, and deliberately lied about her, trying to put her in disfavor with everyone."

"Had you ever taken a look at Caroline, you would understand why George got a snootful on his wedding night," Flavian said, sounding terribly sympathetic toward the Regent. "Ugly doesn't even begin to describe her, and she was coarse and smelly and without morals as well."

"The whole world was scandalized by the goings-on in the royal family," Selina declared, "as well it might be. She did wonderfully well to stay with him for two weeks before leaving him and going to live in Italy."

The mention of Italy seemed to bring other thoughts to her mind and she was quiet for a long time. Finally, she said, "Uncle, as I said before, this is a lot of useless conversation. The Regent already has mistresses a-plenty and no need of more. And as for marrying any of them, it will never happen—not even if Caroline were not still living."

"Should he want to marry again, a way could be found." Flavian nodded wisely.

"I suppose it could," she agreed. "Henry the Eighth certainly found a way, a rather painful way for some of his wives, but nevertheless . . ."

"Oh, Selina, do let's stop this," Flavian begged. "Please try to see the practicality of what I am proposing."

At that moment Daisy came into the room and looked from Flavian to Selina as though wanting an explanation, or perhaps a summation of what had been discussed.

"Aunt, what is your thought on the subject of my becoming a mistress to the Regent?" Selina asked.

"I think . . ." Daisy began, then stopped. She sat down, placed her hands in her lap and then stared at them as though just seeing them for the first time. She had nothing further to say.

Taking her silence to mean that she agreed with Flavian but did not want to say so to her niece, Selina became silent herself. She was tired of the absurdities Flavian was mouthing, tired of the arguing, tired of everything. She gave each of them a long look and then left the room. At least in her bedchamber she could have peace and solitude. She could reflect on what had happened to her and what was going to happen to her without having to listen to Flavian's doltish palavering. Obviously, last night's misadventure had affected him far worse than it had her; he had gone imbecilic.

As she went up the stairs, a knock on the front door caused her to start violently. She stood immobile for a moment, then turned and went back down and answered the door.

In this morning of one shock right after another, she was further shocked to see Aldo Barelli at the door.

Without waiting for him to speak, she greeted him with, "I suppose you have come to apologize for your rag-manners of last evening. Well, I do not feel disposed to accept your apology."

"My dear Miss Bryand," he said, "I do not feel that I have anything for which to apologize. The marriage agreement between my nephew and his fiancée was not

55

made by me and has nothing to do with me. If an apology is owed you, it is owed by Carlo."

She gave him a hard, cold stare and did not answer. Neither did she ask why he had come nor invite him in.

"I have come to ask a great favor of you," he said genially, as though there were no hard feelings on either side. "I would like very much to paint a portrait of you. Would you do me the honor of sitting for me?"

She could not believe she was hearing him correctly, nor did she want to hear him at all. She drew back from the door, and although she did not slam it in his face, she closed it rather firmly.

Five

It was a dreadful night of restlessness, tossing and turning, and, finally, sleep which was just deep enough to produce a harrowing nightmare about the Prince Regent. He was standing over her bed, leering at her, saying lewd things to her which she could not quite hear, and then he bent down as though about to lift the covers and Selina woke herself up screaming.

She was angry at herself for letting Flavian's foolish words about her becoming the Regent's mistress affect her as much as they had. She was positive—almost—that he had not meant what he said, that he had only been trying to get her mind off Carlo and all of her canceled plans. Even if he had been serious, he certainly knew her well enough to know that she most assuredly was not going to become anyone's mistress, least of all a fat, bawdy, ugly man who was old enough to be her father. No matter that he would someday be King (assuming that he outlived his sick, mad father), she did not even want to be in his company, let alone in his bed.

Apparently the Regent had not always been fat and ugly, she thought, remembering a portrait she had seen of him as a young man. He had not been bad-looking; some might even say he had been handsome, but in the portrait his head was held a little too high and there was a haughty look about him. Selina did not like haughty men, not even if they were of the royal family.

But what if Flavian had been serious—as he had sworn he was. He had had wild ideas as long as she had known him, so when he told her his intentions for her, she should not have been too surprised. The surprise was that Daisy agreed with him, was willing for her niece to become not only a woman of low morals but *notorious* as well. It was common knowledge (*very* common) every time the Regent so much as glanced at a woman with that certain look in his eye. Within twenty-four hours all of London knew, by way of the people of the *haut ton* who went to the frequent parties and gatherings at Carlton House, who was and was not bedded by the Regent.

It was early morning and she was as tired as though she had stayed up arguing with Flavian all night. She closed her eyes again, trying to sleep, and finally she did drift off, but she awoke a few minutes later shivering as though with a chill.

She gave up then, got out of bed, dressed, and went down to the cook-room where she made tea and toast. When she finished her solitary breakfast, she went into the small bookroom which contained more of Daisy's collection of glass, rocks, and figurines on the shelves than books. However, she managed to find a book by Wordsworth which she had not yet read. She buried herself in the preface to "Lyrical Ballads," his famous essay which had been published in 1800.

She had not thought she could become so absorbed, her mental condition being what it was, but she was only vaguely aware of noises about the house when Flavian and Daisy came downstairs and went to the breakfast parlor. Later, she realized that Flavian had gone out of the house and Daisy had gone back above stairs, but she did not stop reading until she had finished the essay. Just as she closed the book she heard the front door knocker.

She got up to answer, telling herself that she was safe in doing so for neither Carlo nor his uncle would come back today after the decidedly cool way she had treated each of them yesterday.

She was right; however a third member of the family had now come to see her. She opened the door to find Gemma Moraldo standing outside.

"Gemma!" She did not try to disguise her surprise, though after only a moment's thought it seemed obvious to her why the girl had come. "Are you here to intercede for Carlo or your uncle?" she asked.

"*Aldo?*" Gemma gasped. "Why should I have to intercede for him? And I can tell you most definitely I am not here on Carlo's behalf. He is so witless at handling his own affairs that I am sure he does not deserve *you*, Selina, which is one of the things I came to say to you. But what did you mean about Aldo?"

"He came here yesterday and asked to paint my portrait," Selina said.

"I cannot believe it!" Gemma said. "Yet if you say he came, I must believe it. I had no idea he was here, nor that he had thought of painting you—not that you should not be painted for you are, as Carlo said, the most beautiful girl in the world—one of the few things about which my misguided brother has been correct lately." She stopped suddenly and took a breath, for she had been talking so fast that she had not had time to inhale, and she was beginning to sound like a music box on the verge of running down.

Selina stared at her, not quite knowing what to say to the sister and niece of the two men she loathed.

"Aldo has never before *asked* to paint anyone," Gemma continued after her short breathing spell. "It is always the other way around. Everybody clamors for a portrait done by Barelli. Absolutely everybody! Even the Prince Regent has dropped hints that he would like to be painted by Barelli. It is never necessary for Aldo to ask anyone to pose. But, as I said, I did not come on his behalf or Carlo's. I came for myself. I want us to be friends even though we will not be sisters. I liked you immediately, you know."

Selina smiled, unable to resist the naive, childlike offer of friendship. She stood back from the door and said, "Come in, Gemma."

She took the girl into the drawing room and offered her tea which Gemma accepted with alacrity and, much to Selina's chagrin, followed her to the cook-room and kept up a constant chatter while she made the tea. To Gemma's credit, she never blinked nor acted surprised that Selina made the tea herself or that there were no servants present. Perhaps, Selina thought, Carlo already had told her about the sorry state of things at the house on Half Moon Street. She tried to find out as subtly as possible.

"Did you know that Carlo came here yesterday morning?"

"Yes, he told me after he returned to Grosvenor

Square," Gemma said. "He seemed *disconsolate!* He said you were not very hospitable or nice to him and I asked him what he expected after the way he had treated you by not telling you about Maria and Everything."

Obviously, by the way she said it, the word Everything covered the entire situation and its ramifications in Gemma's mind. "Anyway, he said the two of you had quarreled and there was no possibility of your ever making up, consequently he has no wish to remain in London. He is leaving for Italy tomorrow."

"So soon!" Selina exclaimed. "I hardly expected him to go *that* soon."

"Is it true that the two of you are irreconcilable?" she asked, then immediately answered her own question. "Yes, I suppose it is, because Aldo said so as well as Carlo, and although Carlo may be thickheaded sometimes, Aldo is not. He is always right."

Apparently Selina's horror at the last remark showed plainly on her face, for Gemma said, "He is, Selina. Honestly, he is."

Not wanting to appear churlish to the only member of the family who had treated her decently, Selina gave her a tight little smile and said, "I shall take your word for that," then, in an effort to get the conversation on firmer ground, "Is he going to do a portrait of the Regent?"

"Probably, when there is time. He has already done the Duke of Wellington, you know. And Lord Byron—that is one of my favorites—and he is always painting some member of parliament or nobleman's family. Aldo says Englishmen are far more eager for immortality on canvas than Italians, and that is why he has decided to remain here."

Selina wanted to hear no more about the despised (by

her) and adored (by Gemma) Aldo. It seemed a good time to change the subject. "Shall we take our tea back to the drawing room?"

"No, no," Gemma said, "let us stay here. It is very cozy and informal. I would feel inhibited in my talk with you in the drawing room, and I do want us to be good friends and at ease with each other in spite of . . . What did you tell Aldo? When he asked to paint your portrait, I mean."

"I did not give him an answer," Selina said, not entirely untruthfully, remembering how she had closed the door on him. "How do *you* like London, Gemma? Will you stay here or will you go back to Italy eventually?"

"I wish I will stay here forever," she said. "I feel more at home here now than I do in *Roma*. After all, I have been here for a number of years—not in London, but in England. Carlo and I went to adjoining schools in Cambridge. But London is ever so much bigger, and more social, too. There is always something amusing to do here. For instance . . ." She broke off suddenly and clapped her hands. "Oh, Selina, I have just had a perfectly *splendid* idea. Tomorrow night I am going to Almack's with someone for whom I have developed a real *tendre*—his name is Perry Carwell—and Aldo says I must have a chaperone or else *he* will have to go and he would rather bell a cat than go to Almack's. Why don't you go with us? You could be our chaperone since you are older than I, and we could have the greatest time!"

Selina almost smiled at the enthusiasm which accompanied everything Gemma said or thought, but she shook her head solemnly and declined the invitation. "I am sorry, but I cannot go."

"Why not? Have you already made another engagement for tomorrow? If so . . ."

"I cannot go because I do not have a voucher to Almack's," she explained.

"Then we shall get you one. Aldo will see to that."

"No, it is impossible. My uncle tried two years ago when I first came to London. They will not let me in."

"Well, bad on anyone who tries to keep you out!" Gemma cried, outraged. "You *will* go, Selina. I can get you in and no one will be the wiser."

"No, I . . ."

"It will be simple, the easiest thing in the world. You just leave it to Perry and me and we will get you in. All you have to do is walk right in with us and . . ."

"Gemma, take my word for it, it is impossible. I have heard that the Lady Patronesses are like watchdogs guarding the place to be sure no one is there who shouldn't be."

Gemma was crestfallen. "Don't you trust me, Selina? I thought we were going to be friends. Don't you believe me when I say we can get you in Almack's?"

"I believe you would like to, but . . ."

"Please, Selina, show me that you trust me. Let me try to make up for Carlo's addle-brained behavior," Gemma begged, tears beginning to form in her eyes. "We could have such an incredibly good time, and as I said, no one will ever be the wiser. There is always such a crush in there that no one ever knows, or cares, who is there and who isn't. Please, Selina . . ."

It was terribly hard to say no to such cajoling. It would be like denying a child's innocent wish. Besides, if she *could* get away with it, she might possibly meet just the man she wanted for her "marriage of convenience." After

63

all, she had always heard Almack's described as the marriage mart and certainly that was where the most eligible bachelors in London went looking for the most eligible young ladies.

"Selina, will you?"

There was one more point in favor of acquiescence. If she met a man whom she could marry, then she would hear no more from Flavian about her becoming a mistress to the hideous Prince Regent.

"All right, Gemma," she said. "We will try it. What time tomorrow night should I be ready?"

Six

Selina chose her water-green silk to wear to Almack's because it was the newest gown in her wardrobe and it was the loveliest. Also it was the only one she had ever had which was made by a fashionable *modiste*. However, as she put it on she wondered if perhaps the gown might possibly be bad luck for her. Certainly the only time she had worn it had been anything but a happy occasion. But, being of a practical nature, she did not believe in signs and omens nor even talismans. Since the other night had been disastrous, tonight would be a grand and marvelous occasion to balance the scales.

Daisy, on hearing her plans for the evening, was appalled at first. "Selina, you simply *cannot* go," she declared. "Think how terrible it would be if you were refused entrance, and even if you should get in, there is no assurance that they will let you *stay* in. I have heard . . ."

"Don't push such notions in her head, Daisy," Flavian

interrupted. "I only wish I had thought of sneaking her in myself. Believe me, once the Lady Patronesses see how the men all swarm around Selina, they would think twice before asking her to leave. Good God, it might cause a riot among the men present if they were deprived of their newfound beauty."

Daisy said no more, but Selina could see the worry in her eyes.

Gemma and Perry Carwell arrived promptly at the appointed hour and Gemma, as usual, was bubbling with enthusiasm and high spirits and Mr. Carwell, a clear-eyed young man whose hair was as light as Gemma's was dark, seemed only slightly less euphoric. There was no doubt in their minds that this was to be a night of nights, so whatever remaining doubts Selina had were soon dispelled.

Her nervousness returned, however, when they reached the famed Almack's. Would Gemma be able to get her in or would there be trouble? For a moment, Selina held back, sure that she should not go through with the venture.

"Come on, you ninny," Gemma urged. "There is nothing to worry about. And stop acting so *timid* because that is a dead giveaway. Just walk in as bold as you please, as though you have been coming to Almack's every night of your life. No one will ask you the first question. Just come *on*." Gemma took her hand, half pulling her.

"Gemma is right," Perry said. "Do as she says and everything will go off quite smoothly."

With Perry on one side of her and Gemma on the other, Selina started in. They were no sooner beyond the outer door than Gemma rushed to a group of older ladies and began chattering like a magpie. Selina was about to pause to wait for her but Perry, holding her firmly by the

66

arm, escorted her into a larger room filled with people. They waited just inside the door until Gemma joined them.

"Were they friends of yours?" Selina asked.

"Not exactly," Gemma said, laughing. "Two of them were the Lady Patronesses and the other two were mothers of girls who are here tonight. I wanted to distract them so they would not pay too much attention to you and Perry going in." She seemed very pleased with her successful tactics.

And so was Selina. She began to relax a little and look around her, forming her first impression of Almack's Assembly Rooms as Gemma and Perry showed her about. The rooms were spacious and tastefully done; there was a refinement about them, but there was none of the ornate magnificence which Selina had expected.

Even more than the rooms, Selina was impressed by the people she saw. Never had she seen so many elegantly gowned women and well turned out men assembled in one place. She began to feel like a gawking ninny as she stared, remembering just in time not to let her mouth hang agape.

There were women in pomona-green satin, jaconet muslin, peach muslin with short, puffed sleeves in the latest French mode, Indian mull muslin, garnet satin, white sarsnet trimmed in seed pearls, and primrose gauze gowns. The men all wore exquisitely fitting coats and intricately-tied neckcloths, one or two tied in the *Sentimentale* style. There were black satin knee-breeches and striped silk stockings, waistcoats and pantaloons with silk hose, and a few blue dress coats.

Lost in wonder, Selina hardly noticed Gemma tugging at her arm. "Come," she was saying, "let's go into the ballroom and see how long it takes before you are asked for a dance."

"I predict less than five minutes," Perry said. "And do not worry, Selina. Gemma and I will not desert you until we see that you have a partner."

Selina thanked him and wondered if she would have a partner at all. She could not conceive of anyone, except possibly a close friend of Perry's or Gemma's, asking her to stand up for a dance.

Perry's prediction proved accurate. It was exactly three-and-a-half minutes before a young man approximately Selina's age bowed to her and said, "I am Thon is Rawlson. I do not believe I have had the pleasure of meeting you before."

Perry, though he did not know the man, made the introductions and then Rawlson turned back to Selina. "Would you do me the honor of standing up with me for the set of country dances?"

That was only the beginning of a steady procession of men who tried, through friends, to get an introduction to Selina. Finding that she was not known, they boldly, like Rawlson, introduced themselves and asked her to stand up with them. She was fast becoming the belle of the ball, much sought after for every dance.

Selina had never enjoyed herself more. Her head was spinning and her eyes shining—all of which, according to Gemma and Perry, only made her more beautiful.

They had been in Almack's less than an hour when Selina chanced to look toward the door to the ballroom and saw a man who was quite openly and without embarrassment staring at her. A good many men had stared at her in the short time she had been there, but none in just that way. She stared back, trying to decide if it was bad manners on his part or if, for some reason, he was trying to memorize her in detail.

She lowered her eyes only when he started across the room toward her. He was dressed in dove-colored knee-breeches with black silk hose and a trim fitting black waistcoat. His neckcloth was also of dove-gray. He had brown hair and, she noticed when he reached her side, blue eyes with crinkle lines which indicated to her that he laughed a lot.

"Miss Bryand, my name is Auberon Baldwin and if you would do me the honor of standing up with me for the quadrille, you would make me the happiest of men."

"How did you know my name?" Selina asked, dumbfounded.

He laughed. "I dare say that there is not a man here who has not learned your name. By now, anyone who has not been formally introduced has asked someone who has met you." Without waiting for her answer to his request for the quadrille, he took her arm and led her to the dance floor. She was aware of the gaze of many envious eyes as the dance began, not only the young ladies who obviously would have preferred her partner to their own, but the mothers also who looked at Auberon Baldwin as though he would be the catch of the season.

At the end of the quadrille, Baldwin said to her, "May I hope that you will stand up with me again before the dancing has ended?"

"I should be delighted," Selina said instantly. She had been studying him carefully and had come to the conclusion that, more than anyone she had met so far during the evening, he would qualify for her "marriage of convenience." Not only was he of good social standing—that was evident by the fact that he was here at Almack's (she

69

smiled to herself as she thought of her own devious entrance, but obviously Baldwin was well known and in frequent attendance)—but also he seemed to have all the manners and accouterments of wealth, great wealth. Furthermore, though she could not imagine herself in love with him, neither could she imagine herself ever being revolted by him. He was acceptable to her in every way even though she knew she could never feel about him as deeply as she had about Carlo. Even so, considering how the affair (if one could call it that) with Carlo had turned out, any alliance with Auberon Baldwin was bound to be an improvement.

A little later, at the end of their second dance, he asked if he might escort her in to supper when the time came. Delighted, but not wanting to appear over-eager, she hesitated just a moment before saying, "Yes, I think so. That would be very nice."

At that moment another man, a friend of Perry's, came up to her and claimed her for a waltz. Reluctantly, she went off on his arm, telling Auberon her next dance, the last before supper, was free. He gave her a radiant smile, indicating that it was free no longer.

Selina watched to see whom Auberon would choose for his next partner and was gratified to see that he chose no one, but rather joined a group which appeared to be in earnest conversation on the sidelines. She gave her full attention then to dancing for it was a waltz, her favorite.

As she was whirled around the floor, she noticed out of the corner of her eye two older women looking at her. She realized they were staring at her rather than looking at the dancers in general because their eyes followed her no matter on which side of the ballroom she was. Other eyes watched too, in appreciation of her beauty, her grace, and her expertise in waltzing, but there was no admiration reflected in the eyes of the two women. Their faces held dark scowls. For the first time since those moments right after she entered Almack's, she remembered that she was an intruder here, a trespasser as it were. She was not wanted; she had no right to be here. She felt her face grow red as she became extremely nervous.

Who were those women and, if they so highly disapproved her being here, why had it taken them so long to notice her? She certainly had been no shrinking violet. She had danced every dance, had even had men lined up waiting for a chance to ask her to stand up with them.

Then she remembered seeing the two women when she first came in: they were the ones Gemma had rushed to speak to, the ones she had said were the Lady Patronesses.

Her face grew even redder and she missed a step, causing her partner to step on her toes and then apologize profusely. She hardly heard him.

There was something she remembered hearing a long time ago about waltzing at Almack's, but she could not recall exactly what it was—something about newcomers not being allowed to waltz until they had the permission of the Lady Patronesses. If that was true, she knew why they suddenly were paying attention to her. She was waltzing and they had never laid eyes on her before. Now the two of them were standing close together, quite obviously discussing her.

"Do you mind if we stop?" she asked her partner.

"Are you ill?" He was all concern.

"I do feel a bit faint," she admitted.

He led her back to a chair and asked if he might get

something for her, to which she replied that a glass of water would be lifesaving.

Instantly, she wished that she had not sent him away for no sooner had he left her side than one of the two scowling women approached her. She was a large woman, dressed in rose muslin with mauve ostrich feathers at her neck.

Without preamble, the woman said, "I do not believe we have met, have we?"

"No, ma'am," Selina said at once and then was sorry she had used the subservient ma'am. "I am Selina Bryand."

"Bryand, Bryand," the woman repeated. "I am unfamiliar with that name."

"I have been in London only two years," Selina said. "That is probably why."

"Have you been to Almack's before?"

It was, Selina thought, worse than the Inquisition. She was trying valiantly to maintain her composure, but she wondered where Gemma and Perry were. She needed them—Gemma's glib tongue especially—to come to her rescue.

"This is my first time at Almack's," she admitted, looking the woman straight in the eye. Hoping to divert further questions, she added, "It is a lovely place and I am having a delightful time."

By now others in the vicinity had noticed the Lady Patroness glaring at the belle of the ball and had drawn nearer to hear what was being said. Selina wished that she could drop through the floor. Wildly, she looked around for Gemma and Perry and finally spotted them waltzing on the other side of the room, oblivious to everything and everyone but themselves.

"Bryand, Bryand," the woman said again as though she were taking a lesson in a foreign language. "I do not know anyone in all the town with that name."

"I assure you it *is* my name," Selina said. There was nothing for her to do now but to try to brazen it out. "I came to London to live with my aunt and uncle by marriage two years ago." She realized she was saying more or less the same things over and over, but in her confusion and embarrassment she could think of nothing else.

"And what is the name of your relatives?"

"Curtis. Mr. and Mrs. Flavian Curtis."

The woman looked thoughtful. *"That* name is familiar, I think. Where could I have . . ."

It occurred to both Selina and her questioner at the same time why the name was familiar. Flavian had tried, about a year ago, to get Selina into Almack's. Tried and failed.

By this time all of the people in that part of the room had gathered around to see what was happening and, seeing a group assembled, others stopped dancing to look also. In a matter of minutes it seemed that everyone in Almack's was within earshot of the Inquisition in time to hear the last question to be asked Selina.

"Miss Bryand, am I wrong in thinking that Mr. Curtis sought a voucher for you and failed to get one within the past year?"

Selina stared down at the floor. There was no longer any reason to brazen it out, put up a brave front, or—unless she wanted to out of sheer good manners—even to be civil to the she-dragon who seemed to get such enjoyment out of publicly embarrassing her. Out of the corner of her eye, she could see Gemma and Perry on the periphery of the crowd, unable to get through to her. She

73

also saw Auberon Baldwin standing not too far from her, a look of disgust on his face.

"Would you please answer my question, miss," the she-dragon persisted. "Am I wrong in . . ."

"No, you are not wrong," Selina said softly, her voice scarcely audible even to herself.

"Speak up, please. I cannot hear what you say."

Furious now that this torture should be continued before an audience, Selina looked straight at the woman and said, in tones loud enough to be heard by everyone in the room, "No, you are not wrong. I was denied entrance to Almack's because I could not get a voucher. You see, madam, I come from neither a wealthy nor a titled family and therefore am not socially acceptable . . ."

She was cut off with, "I am afraid I must ask you to leave at once."

"Nothing would give me greater pleasure," Selina said, "if I can just make my way through these gawking spectators."

The crowd parted instantly, like the waters of the Red Sea, making a path for her. She started to go, but turned for one last word to the cause of her humiliation. "*You* may be of impeccable lineage and as plump in the pocket as royalty, madam, but your manners leave much to be desired, and you have a most abrasive and ramshackle way of doing things."

With that, she turned her back on them all and headed for the door. She was nearly out when she heard Gemma calling her name, but she did not stop. For her own sake, she did not want to have to face those smirking people again, and for Gemma's sake she did not want it known that she had come with the girl.

Outside, she found Perry's carriage and asked the driver to take her home.

On the way, she tried not to think about anything, but it was impossible to make her mind a blank. This was the second carriage ride in less than a week which she had made alone because she was running away from an excruciatingly unpleasant experience. But this time she was determined that she would not cry; she was going to be as unemotional as a stone.

She found herself shivering violently, her teeth chattering as though she were in a winter storm without a cloak. She realized it was a nervous reaction, that she felt like exploding inside, but still she would not let herself cry. Never again would she shed a tear over the *haut ton* or anyone who was part of it.

However, there was one thought she could neither ignore nor forget: It was all her own fault. Had she not put herself in such a position by going where she was not wanted, there would have been no dreadful scene, no crippling embarrassment. Would she never learn?

She had left Aldo Barelli's house because she felt she was an unwanted outsider. Now she had been asked to leave Almack's for the very same reason.

Her first impulse was to blame Flavian for wanting her to rise above what he called their "situation in life," but she knew it was not entirely his fault. She had enjoyed the parties, the pretty clothes, the attentions of well-situated men. The truth was, she had had the time of her life tonight until it was discovered that she had no right to be there.

Now she was beginning to understand the progression of Flavian's thoughts and how he finally arrived at the conclusion that she should be a mistress to the Prince Regent. (Her own plan of a "marriage of convenience—her convenience" had been discarded the moment she saw the look of disgust on Auberon Baldwin's face.) Actually, unless she wanted to marry some clerk—or worse, a ne'er-do-well—and spend her life bearing and rearing his children and being a household drudge and never having quite enough of anything—food, clothing, respect, love— her only alternative was to become the mistress of a wealthy man.

And if she was going to become a mistress, it might as well be to Prinny as anyone else.

At least *his* mistresses were never asked to leave *any* party, and neither were they hidden away as though they had contracted the plague and were unfit to associate with healthy people.

At this point, she did not care about anything, not anything at all, and as long as she could remain numb, perhaps being Prinny's mistress would not be so distasteful to her.

Tomorrow morning she would tell Flavian that she had given serious thought to his idea and was willing to try it, provided he could bring about a meeting with the licentious Lothario.

Seven

  Daisy had his breakfast waiting for him when Flavian went to the breakfast parlor. He was hoping that Selina would be up, but apparently she was still asleep for he had heard no sound from her room. He was all agog with curiosity, eagerness and anxiety. How had it gone at Almack's last night? Would there be swains flocking to the house now like sloe-eyed sheep, sick with love? He prayed it would happen just so.

  "I wonder how long Selina will sleep," Daisy said.

  "I take it as a good sign," Flavian replied. "The fact that she is still asleep indicates that she was very late coming home, and that indicates she was having a grand time . . . I didn't hear her come in, did you?"

  "Yes, but I do not know what time it was, I was asleep and I woke up when I heard the front door close."

  "I am surprised you did not rush to her to get an account of the night right then."

  "I went back to sleep," Daisy confessed.

They finished their breakfast and were having a second cup of coffee in the bookroom when Selma came downstairs.

"Good morning," Daisy cried out to let her know where they were. She got up and went out into the hall just as Selina reached the bottom of the stairs. "I will get your breakfast for you."

"No, go back to your coffee," Selina said. "That is all I want and I will get it."

"I suppose the late supper at Almack's has taken your appetite for breakfast," Daisy said.

"Certainly *something* at Almack's has taken my appetite," Selina agreed.

"Bring your coffee into the bookroom," Daisy said and went back to Flavian.

"What sort of mood is she in?" he asked immediately.

"I am not sure. I think she might have eaten something that did not agree with her."

"A small price to pay if everything else turned out well," Flavian observed.

However, when Selina came into the bookroom, he knew instantly that something had gone wrong last night, very wrong. She looked pale and drawn, as though she had had no sleep for weeks. There were dark circles beneath her eyes and even tiny worry wrinkles about her mouth. Good God, that would never do! She would make herself into an ugly old woman before she could take advantage of her youth and beauty!

"What happened?" he asked dully, still hoping for the best but knowing he was going to hear the worst.

"I was asked to leave." There was no emotion whatever in the words; in a monotone, she had merely made a statement of fact.

"*What?*" Daisy cried. "That cannot be. I understood that the Moraldo girl expected to have no trouble at all in getting you in Almack's."

"There was no trouble getting in," Selina said, "the trouble was in *staying* in. I called attention to myself by waltzing without the permission of the Lady Patronesses and one of them questioned me and found out I had no right to be there."

"Do you mean she literally asked you to leave, or did you just become uncomfortable and decide to go?" Flavian asked. In his opinion, it would make a great deal of difference.

"Her words were, 'I am afraid I must ask you to leave at once.' Judge for yourself."

"Oh, my dear!" Daisy's sympathy had her on the verge of tears. "What did you do?"

"I left, of course."

Flavian did not like the exceedingly calm tone of voice in which Selina was relating the atrocities of last night. She should be upset, or angry, or bitter, or resentful. She should *not* be calm and act as though she were talking about someone she hardly knew.

"What happened to the couple you went with?" he asked. "Did they desert you when they saw you in trouble?"

"No, I deserted them," Selina said. "I did not want to get them in trouble for having taken me to Almack's in the first place."

"Did no one see or hear what was happening?" Daisy asked. "Wasn't there anyone to champion your cause?"

"Everyone there saw and heard everything," Selina said. "You can believe that my disgrace is on the tip of every tongue in London this morning."

"Oh, my dear sweet Lord," Flavian murmured, seeing an end to all of his hopes, plans, and dreams for the future. The three of them would live and die in penury.

"I have decided, Uncle," Selina said, her monotone changing to one of deepest solemnity, "that the best course for me is to abide by your decision. I am no longer unwilling to become the Regent's mistress—that is, if you can think of a way to bring it about."

Flavian could not believe he was hearing aright. And if he was, then she must have suddenly gone all about in her head. After all of her vehement objections, it seemed impossible that she was now relenting and saying that what she had previously thought to be unspeakably wrong was now what she considered "the best course for me."

One thing he did know for certain: if she was of a mind to go through with it, he had better do what he could to get the affair—he smiled at his own choice of words—launched before she changed her mind. Knowing Selina, her current mood and compliant manner would not be with her long.

"I think you have come to a wise decision, me gel," he said, ignoring Daisy's frown. "I shall put my mind to work right away to come up with a way of getting you into Carlton House. That is . . ."

"No!" Selina shouted. "No, no, no!"

Flavian looked at her in wonder. He had never known a woman to change her mind *that* quickly before.

"I shall never again go anywhere that I am not invited," Selina continued. "Never! No one will ever have reason to ask me to leave any place on earth. If you cannot think of a way for me to meet the Regent without having to sneak me in somewhere uninvited, we can just forget this whole sorry business."

Flavian put his coffee cup down and began to pace around the small room. "I shall think of a way to get you an invitation then. But I do not think you should equate Carlton House with Almack's. As I have told you repeatedly, once Prinny claps his orbs on you, the rest will be history. And Daisy, me gel, you and I will be watching history in the making. Our Selina will go down as one of the great beauties of all time and, who knows?, she may even play a part in the course of events of the government."

When he had begun talking, he had been fresh out of hope, on the brink of total despondency, however his words cheered him immensely and by the time he finished, he was feeling much better about the prospects for their future.

Apparently Daisy and Selina did not share his optimism, judging from the expressions on their faces. Daisy looked both dubious and disgusted and Selina looked as though she had gone off into another world and saw and heard nothing of the one in which she had current residence.

Something else he knew for certain was that he would have to get some money, not only for their everyday expenses, but also for more new gowns for Selina and perhaps to pay for a few favors. His mind already at work, it did not seem inconceivable that he could meet someone who worked for the Regent, a valet or butler or—if no better—maybe even a cook or cleaner. Any of those should be able to give him some idea of how to get Selina into Carlton House at one of Prinny's gatherings—and maybe, if he were extraordinarily lucky, he could get one of the servants to steal an invitation before it was sent out to someone else. If a pile of them were left lying somewhere before being delivered . . . There were all kinds of possibilities, and he needed to go over them one by one in his mind. But first, he needed money.

"I must go out for a while," he said. "I may be gone most of the day."

Just the thought of what he was about to do made him suffer great fatigue, but no matter how much he hated it, he would have to spend the day at cards to finance Selina's—and his and Daisy's—future.

At St. James Square was an old house which had been changed into a gaming-hell where the young men of the *ton* found amusement of an evening. However, those who gambled for more than momentary entertainment often were seen entering and leaving during daylight hours. These were the card players who took their card playing—and winnings and losses—quite seriously.

Flavian had been taken to this particular house by a young man of the *ton* who had lost to him in a much less fashionable gaming-hell and could not pay his losses without alerting his father to the fact that he was heavily in debt from gambling. Flavian knew that once he was introduced at the house by a gentleman of quality, he would be able to return as often as he liked. He also knew that he would not be returning often enough to make anyone either suspicious or unduly pensive about his great winnings. He went so infrequently that he rarely saw the same players twice in a row.

Although he had never been there this early in the day before, he was, nevertheless, surprised to find the house almost deserted. He went from the large card room which seemed cavernous because of is emptiness, into the smaller room. At first he thought that it, too, was empty. The shades were drawn, as always, and only one lamp was lit so he did not see the one man present in the semi-darkness. A loud "Harrumph!" caused him to look toward a table in the corner.

"I have been wondering how long I would have to sit here before I was blessed with company." A tall stately-looking man stood up and held out his hand. "Lord Hanley Baldwin at your service, sir. Could I interest you in a little game?"

"Flavian Curtis," he shook the man's hand, "and that is exactly why I am here."

That was the end of the amenities, the end of any conversation whatsoever. It was seldom that Flavian had ever come across a player like Lord Hanley Baldwin. He kept his mouth shut so tight that he seemed to be biting his lips together, his eyes opened so wide that, were they not focused, Flavian would have felt the man's pulse, and his hands, holding the cards, were rigid and white-knuckled. They were, Flavian thought, like something carved out of granite. He had been so absorbed with these features that he had almost forgotten a matter of critical importance.

"The stakes?" he said.

"Stakes? Ah, yes, the stakes." Lord Baldwin murmured. "Let's just make it a friendly little game, something that won't hurt either of us too much." And then he proceded to name the highest stakes Flavian had ever played for. He did not flinch though, and agreed at once, for the higher the stakes, the less time he would have to spend here. If he played his usual good game, he could be home well before midafternoon.

He picked up his cards and looked at them, for a moment imagining that he was playing with the Prince Regent. He had no idea whether Prinny was good at cards or, for that matter, even played at all, but it gave him an unaccustomed feeling of power just to imagine himself in Carlton House. And that was where he would be as soon as Selina had established herself in Prinny's good graces.

His mind returned to his thoughts of earlier that morning: how to bring Selina to the attention of the prince. He could think of no way except to get her into Carlton House. That was the only place one could be sure of seeing the prince and of being seen by him.

He looked across the board at his opponent and almost laughed at the deep study registered on his face.

He himself had just lost a game or two, but he did that sometimes before he tightened his concentration and took his opponent by surprise, winning everything.

His mind went back to Selina. He was terribly sorry that she had had such a bad time of it last night, but perhaps in the long run it was for the best. Having been brought up in modest circumstances, it was possible that she might not feel too much at ease with the crowd who went to Almack's. Then it would reasonably follow that, that being the case, she would feel even less at ease with the Carlton House set, but Flavian knew that this was erroneous thinking. At Carlton House she would be almost like the hostess. And . . . oh, joyous thought! . . . if the Prince became really enamored of Selina, it was entirely possible that someday she might indeed be hostess. As he had told Selina, royalty had a way of getting what it wanted. If Prinny wanted her for his wife, he could find a way to make it possible.

Flavian wondered briefly about the state of Caroline's health and if she would consider returning to England once Prinny became King. She would, of course. He was sure of that. No woman would turn down a chance to be crowned Queen of England.

But there was no comparison between Selina and Caroline. It was like comparing a peahen to a mudhen.

He cringed when he realized that he was still losing. The expression on Lord Baldwin's face now was more relaxed, something between a smile and a smirk.

His Lordship stood up, stretching. "That's enough for now. I don't like to sit too long at a time. Problems of circulation, you know."

"But, but we only just started," Flavian protested.

"Only just started! My good man, do you realize that we have been playing for nearly two hours? And I must say you are a formidable player. I would like to take you on again sometime." He passed a piece of paper across to Flavian.

Flavian looked at it. "What is this?"

"Your losses, sir. Since you did not seem to be keeping account, I decided I had better do it for you."

Flavian looked at the paper again. It wasn't possible. It was more money than he had in the world, more than he would ever be able to borrow. Why in the name of heaven had he not kept his mind on the game instead of on Selina and her concerns?

"We must play again?" Flavian insisted. "We must make an engagement for . . . say, tomorrow?"

"Not tomorrow, I am afraid," the now broadly smiling man said good-naturedly. "But I am sure we shall have another chance meeting sometime. I come here every month or so when I get the urge for a little game. Mostly, though, I go to White's."

Flavian knew that he had as much chance getting into

White's for a little game as Selina had of getting back into Almack's for a little dance.

"But—but . . ." He did not know what to say next. He had never been in this situation before.

"Don't worry about paying me right this minute," Lord Baldwin said magnaminously. "I shall be happy to take either your check or your note."

"I do not seem to have a check with me."

"Your note will be fine."

Which Flavian had to give him; there was no other way.

He walked home so it would take longer and he could think. Since neither Daisy nor Selina knew he was a card player, he had nothing to explain, but he had to try to think of some way to win back his losses from Lord Hanley Baldwin. Yet even as he walked and thought, walked and thought, he knew he would never on the longest day he lived be able to get his hands on that much money.

Eight

'After Flavian left the house on whatever mysterious errand had caused him to go with such dispatch, Selina and Daisy went outside to marvel at the sudden change in the weather. The unseasonable cold spell had gone, and the air was warm and fragrant with the odors of spring.

"Thank heavens," Daisy breathed. "The older I become the gladder I am to see springtime every year. Selina, let's go for a walk."

"I'd rather not," Selina said, thinking how terrible it would be if she should chance to see someone who had been at Almack's last night.

"Oh, come on," Daisy urged. "It will do you good. You certainly can't want to stay inside that gloomy house on such a day as this."

"There are . . . some things that need my attention." The excuse sounded lame even to Selina. She gave Daisy a weak smile and said, "Some other time, Aunt—but you go ahead and have your walk. It *is* a lovely day."

"I always feel that on days like this nothing very bad could happen," Daisy said. "I think I shall go to see my friend Margaret Seabrook. She lives nearby, you know."

Finding Daisy's optimism a bit sickening in her present frame of mind, Selina hurried back into the house. There was, of course, nothing she had to do except to fret over the outcome of last evening. She could not stop berating herself for her stupidity in letting Gemma—dear, impulsive, brash Gemma—talk her into doing such an addle-brained thing.

She went to the bookroom and picked up the Wordsworth book she had been reading the other day, but it did not hold her now as it had then. She could not get her mind off her misery of the past as well as that which was to come in the future.

She tried a novel, but that was no better. Finally, discarding the idea of trying to read, she began to pace the small room like an untamed, caged animal unaccustomed to the confines of a civilized world. And she was still at it twenty minutes later when she heard the great knocker at the front door.

Daisy, she thought, unable to get in. However, when she opened the door, it was a strangely solemn-faced Gemma who stood there.

"Oh, Selina, I am *desolate* about what happened!" Gemma cried and embraced her as though consoling her on a death in the family. "How can I *ever* stop apologizing for getting you into such a scrape? Do you think you can ever forgive me? Oh, please, I shall *die* right now if you tell me you will hate me forever, even though you have every right to."

In spite of herself, Selina laughed. "Come in, Gemma, and stop groveling. Nothing is worth *that* much desolation. Besides, last night was my fault, not yours. I never should have gone. I knew better, but . . ."

"No, I will not let you blame yourself for it was I who *implored* you to go. But, believe me, Selina, I *never* expected anything like that to happen. Never! I thought we would have a nice evening and then go home. I thought it would be uneventful—except that maybe you would meet someone who could replace Carlo. I thought I owed you that since Carlo is my brother and he behaved so badly toward you."

The smile left Selina's face as she thought: Of course, it is Carlo who is more to blame for what happened than anyone else, for if he had not jilted me, I never would have been put in such a ramshackle position. Carlo and the abominable Aldo.

She looked down the street as a carriage went by and said, "Let's not stand here at the door for every passerby to gaze upon."

"No, I cannot stay inside on the first gorgeous day of the season. Let's go to the park. Raymond, my coachman, can follow us in the carriage until we get tired of walking and then we can ride."

"No!" Selina drew back. "I—I do not feel like walking."

"Then we shall ride," Gemma said.

"No, I do not feel like going out at all." Selina put her hands to her head as though severe pain had come to take permanent residence in her temples.

"You *must* go out," Gemma insisted. "Don't be a ninny, Selina. You cannot expect to spend the rest of your life in seclusion just because those old witches behaved shamefully last night. Come on. You must show people that . . ."

"No, Gemma, I will not go through the park, walking or riding. We are sure to see someone who would recognize me and that would put you in an untenable position."

"Selina, you are enough to make me curse like an ostler. The thing to do is *see* people, as many as you can as soon as you can. If they look at you, then you outstare them. If you go into hiding that will make everyone think you were trying to get away with something last night and failed miserably."

"And that," Selina said, "is precisely what happened."

"Well, maybe, but you don't have to fly into the boughs over it." She took Selina's hand and pulled her outside. "Now, we shall go to the park."

What did it matter whether she walked in the park or stayed at home? Nothing was going to cheer her up and nothing was going to make people forget what had happened last night, so if seeing her and having something else to talk about made people happy, then she would, she thought sarcastically, be glad to contribute her part to their *on dits*.

"All right," she said to Gemma, "if it doesn't bother you to be seen with me, then it doesn't bother me to be seen."

They rode in Aldo Barelli's carriage to the edge of the park and then got out, telling Raymond to wait there for them while they took a turn about the park.

At first Selina walked with her eyes down as though searching out poisonous snakes lest she step on one. Her mind was on anything but Gemma's prattle until she realized that Gemma was talking about what had happened at Almack's after Selina left.

90

". . . and everyone thought it was simply horrid of the Lady Patronesses to ask you to leave the way they did. Perry and I heard talk about it from all sides. And, oh, Selina! you should have heard what some of the *handsomest* men had to say about it! One standing near me said quite plainly, 'The most beautiful girl who has ever come to Almack's and that old crow had the gall to ask her to leave. It's the *old* girl who should be drummed out of Almack's.' Everyone thought . . ."

"The Patronesses were only doing what they were supposed to do," Selina interrupted. "I should not have been there."

"Just let me finish, will you?" Gemma said. "Everyone thought it was done in a most *appalling* manner. The old crow should merely have whispered to you whatever she had to say and let you go out quietly and . . ."

"It's over now," Selina said, "and it is no good talking about it. Talk will not change anything."

She resumed looking at the ground and trying to get her mind on something else.

"You are right. We must talk of more cheerful things. Oh, look over there!" Gemma pointed toward a carriage that had stopped while a curricle pulled alongside. "That is Lady Caroline Lamb's carriage so that must be Byron. Selina, we are witnessing an assignation! Isn't it exciting!"

"It's only another woman she is talking to," Selina said as they drew abreast of the two vehicles. "Besides, the Byron affair ended long ago."

"Poor thing, she looks *desolated*," Gemma said. "Wouldn't it be the other side of *entrancement* to have an affair with someone like Byron?"

"Why ever would you want to?" Selina asked. "I imagine there are quite a few women who would tell you that there is no one *like* Byron when it comes to having their reputations ruined. You would probably look desolated too if you were in Lady Caro's place."

"But I wouldn't *be* desolated," Gemma said emphatically. "Not after having an affair with a romantic figure like Byron or an important man like . . ." She hesitated, trying to think of a man important enough to deserve her attention.

"How would you feel about the Prince Regent?" Selina ventured.

"Ugh!" was the first reaction, then, "we-ell, I am not sure. Prinny *is* important, and maybe beneath all that fat he is attractive and the charming ladies' man everyone says he is, but . . ." She paused again for a moment, then said, "No, it would be all right. It would *have* to be all right because he is the *King*, you know—at least, he will be when the old King dies—and no woman would ever turn down a chance for her name to be linked romantically with that of the King, even if he's ugly."

"Gemma, you are a hopeless romantic," Selina sighed.

Gemma laughed. "You have it worded wrong, Selina. As long as I am a romantic, nothing is hopeless."

If Gemma said anything after that, Selina did not hear it for at that moment she looked up and saw a couple, arm in arm, approaching them. She had never seen the girl before, an attractive young lady whose bright muslin dress matched exactly her coppery curls, but she recognized the man instantly. It was Auberon Baldwin.

She felt tentacles of panic clutching at her lungs so that she could not breathe, and she felt her face redden with the remembered shame of last night. Auberon, who had asked to be her supper partner at Almack's, had stood silently watching while she had been evicted from the premises. He certainly could not have liked it above half that he had been so attentive to someone who was *persona non grata*.

It was too late to turn away or to cross to the other side of the carriage road as though she had not seen him. She did not know what to do, whether to pass him as though they had never met or to speak to him as though they were, or had been, friends. Finally, deciding that her course lay somewhere in between, she smiled and nodded to him as he and the girl went by.

She wished immediately that she had ignored him, for he gave her a curt nod, looking embarrassed, and walked on without speaking. She felt crushed; never had she been so snubbed, so put in her place.

"Do you know them?" Gemma asked as soon as they were out of earshot. "He looked as though he wasn't sure whether he knew us or not."

"I have seen him before somewhere," was all that Selina said. Obviously, Gemma had not seen him dancing with her last night. In her mind, she went through the whole humiliating evening again, especially the terrible scene which was witnessed by all there. If it had not happened, if the curcumstances had been different, *she* might be the girl walking with Auberon Baldwin in the park today.

"We must turn around," she said to Gemma. "I have to go home now."

"But we've hardly walked at all!"

"I'm sorry, but I . . . must get home."

"All right, but will you have dinner with us tonight?"

"Us?" Selina asked, thinking Gemma meant Perry.

"Aldo and me. At Grosvenor Square."

Selina felt herself bristle like an angry cat. "Thank you,

Gemma. I know you mean well, but I have no wish to see your atrocious uncle again, and if you and I are to remain friends, I advise you not even to mention his name to me."

The day, which had begun so unpromisingly, was continuing in the same vein.

Nine

It might as well be the end of the world as far as he was concerned; it was certainly the end of *his* world. The closer he came to the house, the more he wanted to turn back toward the Thames and walk into the river until his hat floated.

He had given Lord Baldwin his note for more money than he had on earth, and he could not tell either Daisy or Selina his troubles because neither knew that he gambled and he did not want them ever to find out. Besides, it would do no good at all if they did find out because *they* could not pay off his debts—that is, unless he could bring Selina to the Prince Regent's attention at once. He could, he supposed, get into another game, but the way he felt now, he would only lose more than he had just lost to Baldwin.

Flavian's spirits had never been so low. When he reached the house on Half Moon Street he stood outside for a moment looking at it as though appraising its worth.

He had won the house at cards; it seemed likely he would lose it the same way. The house of cards, he thought. Ironic, but not funny. He could not afford to lose anything, least of all the house. And what will Cock Robin do then, poor thing? The line of the old nursery verse came to mind. It seemed a lot of foolishness was seeping into his thoughts now and he wondered if the shock of losing at cards was causing him to lose his mind.

He went inside very quietly, hoping that he would see neither of the women. This, however, as had already been proved, was not to be his most fortunate day. Selina was in the drawing room, seated in the large wing chair, staring into the stone fireplace as though expecting something remarkable to happen there. Since there was no fire, Flavian could not imagine what it was that so held her interest. He could see only her profile, but she appeared to be no happier than he.

She looked up just as he was about to go by the door. "Uncle, you missed lunch, but Aunt is still in the cookroom so perhaps she will prepare something for you."

"I am not hungry," he said, then deliberately lied in order to avoid further conversation on the subject. "I have eaten already."

"Is something wrong?" Selina asked. "You seem rather agitated."

"I could well make the same observation about you," he replied.

"Just so," she admitted, "but you know what is troubling me, while I am very much in the dark as to what might be bothering you."

And that was where he wanted to keep her, and Daisy also: very much in the dark. He went into the drawing room and sat down opposite her. He wondered how she would react if he told her he had just lost a fortune at cards. Would she be scandalized (he was sure Daisy would) or would she be sympathetic?

At any rate, he had no idea of finding out which. That was one chance he did not think it necessary to take right now. Yet he would have to tell her something for it was she who could help him out of his difficulties and he needed that help at once for he had no idea when Baldwin would demand payment of the note.

"I do have a rather pressing worry right now." He spoke *sotto voce* so there would be no possibility of Daisy overhearing. "A bit of financial trouble."

"What is it?" Selina asked when he did not seem disposed to go on.

"The money that was left to me at the same time this house was is getting low." There, it was out; at least that much was out, but he did not feel much better for having made the admission.

"How low?" Selina asked.

"Quite low."

She looked at him steadily. "How low is quite low, Uncle?"

The prince in a pushcart! Couldn't she let it alone now that he had made his self-deprecating confession that he was a man of no means?

"*How* low, Uncle?" she repeated.

"Dangerously low," he said, "but I do not want Daisy to find out yet. No need for her to worry until it is absolutely necessary."

"I agree, but I still have no idea . . ."

"I think we must find a way for you to meet the Prince quickly—very quickly," he interrupted.

"Is it that bad, Uncle? Are we in such straits?"

97

He nodded, unable to speak.

"Then perhaps I should consider looking for work somewhere. Perhaps as an abigail or . . . surely there must be something I can do."

"There is," he said, "and it has nothing to do with some menial servant's job, or even a position as a governess. You must find a way to get inside Carlton House where you will come to the attention of the Regent."

"I can think of no way," she said, "unless perhaps I can find work there. Surely in that vast place they must always be looking for maidservants or . . ."

Again, he would not let her finish. "In the first place, you know nothing about that sort of work, and in the second place, you would have no chance of being employed at Carlton House even if you did."

"But, Uncle, it is the only way I can think of that would give me an excuse to go inside the Prince's residence."

"It will not do at all," he assured her. "If you get to Prinny that way, it would lessen you considerably in his estimation. Surely you do not think he has to pick his mistresses from among his servants."

"It would not be unheard of. I have . . ."

"Cite me no examples to the contrary," he said. "You must be presented to him as a lady of quality."

She looked at him then, and had her eyes not been so troubled, he was sure he would have noticed a slight twinkle as she said, "And how do you propose to arrange that?"

"It would help if you would *think* of yourself as quality," he told her. "You are a lady of quality whether you know it or not. One has only to look at you to realize that. The fact that you may not be as highborn as some in

Prinny's set does not keep you from acting like a lady, and one of high quality at that."

"Those close to the Fat One's court would not go along with your reasoning."

"For the love of heaven, Selina, do not refer to him as the Fat One. You might slip sometime."

"Believe me, Uncle, were I in his presence, there is not the slightest possibility that I would refer to him as anything but Your Majesty."

Daisy came into the room then. "I thought I heard voices in here. What are you afraid Selina is going to say, Flavian?"

"I am afraid her careless tongue is going to put a rapid end to our plan for her before it even has a chance to start," he said.

"*Our* plan!" Daisy gave him a hard look.

Flavian ignored her. "Selina and I were just trying to think of a way to get her into Carlton House as soon as possible. I had thought of a way—getting to know one of the household staff and having him pilfer an invitation to a party or ball—but that would take much too long."

"Why the need to rush?" Daisy asked.

"Er, I cannot . . . it just seems to me that it would be better to go ahead with the plan, especially now that the weather has turned so pleasant."

"And just what may the weather have to do with it?" Daisy looked perplexed.

"It is springtime, woman!" Flavian appeared to be losing his patience at such a tottyheaded question. "The Prince will be easier to . . ." He paused, searching for a word.

"Seduce." Selina supplied the word.

"What I meant was, most people are more vulnerable to love during the spring, even those of Prinny's age."

"I think we had better wait until after we are introduced before you predict Prinny's reaction to me," Selina said.

"He is going to fall top-over-tail in love with you," Flavian said, "and if I were a gambling man I would wager a considerable sum on it."

"And you might lose that considerable sum, too," Selina said.

Flavian cringed noticeably. He tried to recover by saying, "Who knows but what Prinny may become as enamored of you as he did of Mrs. Fitzherbert?"

"Who knows, indeed," Daisy said grimly.

Ten

A day passed and then another and another, but to two of the residents of the house on Half Moon Street, the adage that time heals all wounds held no meaning. For both of them, the passage of time was still another reason to panic. For Flavian, every day that went by meant that the time was nearer when Baldwin would call for payment of the note. For Selina, each day put her one day closer to the time when she must meet the Regent—and there was no doubt in her mind that Flavian would, sooner or later, find a way to bring about that much dreaded meeting. She knew she would have to go through with it and, should she take the Prince's fancy, meet him again and again.

That was the least—and the most—she could do for Flavian and Daisy.

Daisy was the one member of the household who remained only moderately perturbed. She knew nothing of Flavian's dilemma, therefore she thought the furrows in his brow were caused by Selina's situation. Although she did not approve of Flavian's plan to try to make Selina the Prince's mistress, she did not openly express disapproval, for she was convinced that, first of all, he would never find a way to bring Selina to His Majesty's attention and, secondly, even if he did, that did not necessarily mean that anything would come of the meeting. In all probability, the Prince Regent had beautiful girls presented to him every day. He certainly could not take *all* of them to bed, gossip to the contrary.

Occasionally at mealtime, she would see Flavian and Selina catch each other's eye across the table and a significant look would pass between them. However, she had no idea what that look signified. She had asked "Do you two have a secret?" Selina had given a harsh, false laugh and said, "Yes, Aunt, the Prince has obtained a divorce from Caroline and has offered for me," whereupon Flavian muttered, "Would to God it were true."

Daisy then looked from one to the other and said, "I find your sense of humor somewhat distorted."

"As far as I can see," Flavian said, "The times are distorted. Nothing is the way it was."

"And it never will be again," Selina added.

Daisy decided not to pursue the matter further; she would let well enough alone. If they were sharing a private joke (which she doubted because of their grim countenances) that was fine, and if it had something to do with Flavian's nefarious scheme, she would rather not know about it.

There were also certain facts which Selina did not care to know. She never questioned Flavian about any possible progress made in his "plan." She supposed that he would let her know the minute he had something arranged. Unlike Daisy, she was positive that eventually Flavian would bring about that meeting. If he could think of no other way, he probably would have her step in front of the royal carriage as a means of getting the Regent's attention. The method seemed extreme, but then, many of Flavian's methods were.

At mid-morning a week after Selina's walk in the park and chance meeting with Auberon Baldwin which had so upset her, Gemma came to see her. She was her usual ebullient self, and no sooner was she seated in the drawing room than she started right in, excitedly, "Selina, you can never imagine what has happened!"

"I would not even try," Selina replied, her interest at half-mast in spite of Gemma's high spirits.

Gemma calmed down somewhat. "Perhaps I should begin at the beginning instead of stupefying you right off," she said. "I am still reproaching myself for that horrible evening at Almack's, and I have tried and tried to think of a way to make up to you for the embarrassment I unwittingly caused."

"But I have told you over and over that it was not your fault," Selina protested. "I should have known better than to go to Almack's."

"We won't argue now over whose fault it was or wasn't," Gemma went on, her dark eyes seeming to flash sparks. "The point is, I have found a way to make it up to you—that is, Aldo has."

Selina stiffened in her chair. "Gemma, I thought I made it clear to you that I am not an admirer of your uncle and I do not want to discuss him or even mention his name."

"Oh, Selina, do listen, and stop sounding as though you have windmills in your head. Please don't speak again until I tell you what has happened." Gemma then took a deep breath and proceeded. "Aldo has received an invitation to a party at Carlton House, and Carlo and I were included!"

"How nice," Selina said. If there was anyone she would less rather hear about than the abominable Aldo it was the cowardly Carlo.

Gemma looked at her seriously, then laughed. "You ninnyhammer, have you not caught on yet? Since Carlo has gone, Aldo can invite someone to go in his place. He can take two 'nieces' instead of a niece and a nephew."

"I should think you would invite Perry Carwell to replace Carlo."

"I want you to go," Gemma said. "Come on, Selina, please say you will."

Selina was almost stunned by the irony of it all. Here Flavian was practically fragmenting his brain trying to find a way to get her into Carlton House, and little Gemma was offering her an invitation as though it were an everyday occurrence—but under circumstances that made the invitation completely unacceptable.

"Your uncle would fly up into the boughs if he knew you had invited me," she said.

"No, not at all," Gemma assured her. "Aldo himself said it would be all right. I asked him as soon as I saw the invitation and he said I could invite you to go in Carlo's place. In fact, he seemed to think it a marvelous idea."

"Did he say that?"

"Well, no, but I could tell he thought so."

"Gemma, you are impossible! Don't you know you could get in trouble by taking someone who isn't invited?"

"It will be a squeeze, Aldo says," Gemma explained. "There will be so many people that no one will know who

104

is there and who isn't. Anyway, Aldo's invitation is for three people and three people will go."

"I thank you for thinking of me," Selina said, "but I could not possibly go with you and your uncle." She did not want to make any more derogatory remarks about Aldo Barelli to his niece, but it was hard to refrain when she felt so strongly about him.

"Is it because of Aldo that you won't say yes?" Gemma asked.

"I find I am able to keep my enthusiasm for him within bounds."

Gemma sighed. "But, Selina, he will find some of his friends as soon as we get there, and we shall be left to our own devices. Just think, the two of us at Carlton House!"

Selina was again about to decline with thanks when Flavian and Daisy came into the room. Without even waiting for a proper greeting, Gemma cried, "Oh, Mr. and Mrs. Curtis, I need your help. Please tell Selina that she is wrong to refuse and that she should go with us."

"Wrong to refuse what?" Flavian asked.

"Gemma just gave me an invitation which I cannot possibly accept," Selina said, hoping to end the conversation right there.

"Where is it you are going?" Daisy asked.

"My uncle has been invited to a squeeze by Prinny and he can take two people with him. We want to take Selina, but she . . ."

"Is this a gathering where the Prince will be present?" Flavian asked, incredulous.

"Yes, at Carlton House next week, and . . ."

"And Selina *refused* your invitation?" Flavian stared at Selina now, even more incredulous.

"I refused because it would mean going with Aldo

Barelli," Selina said hastily, trying to let Flavian know the reasoning behind her refusal before he said something that would be better left unsaid. "It was Mr. Barelli who insisted that Carlo go back to Italy, if you remember. It was he who . . ."

"That is in the past," Flavian interrupted, his face becoming a haven for gathering thunderheads, "and the past is *forgotten*. We have to think about the *future* now, don't we, Selina?" He loosed the thunderheads in her direction.

She lowered her head and did not answer. She would, if absolutely necessary, go through with her promise to do what she could to attract the Prince, but she simply could not bring herself to get to the Prince by way of Aldo Barelli. As repulsive as she thought the Regent to be, her opinion of him was high compared to her opinion of Barelli.

"It would be so much more enjoyable for me if you would go, Selina," Gemma insisted. "Please say you will."

Still Selina said nothing, but Flavian answered for her. "There is no doubt about her going. She *will* go." He looked straight at Selina, emphasizing his words.

Daisy, who had remained quiet through it all, now spoke up. "But Flavian, if Selina thinks it best not to go this time . . ."

"*This* time!" Flavian was almost shouting. "You sound as though she gets an invitation to Carlton House every day. Don't you realize that this is what we have been trying . . ." He stopped, obviously catching himself before he revealed to Gemma just how much he had wanted that invitation for Selina.

"All right," Selina said finally, knowing that she could do nothing else. "I will go."

Gemma clapped her hands like an excited child. "It

106

will be a splendid occasion, a night we will remember all our lives!"

"I have had two nights recently that I will remember all my life," Selina said drily, "and I believe I can manage to exist without another such night."

"You will enjoy it excessively," Gemma declared. "Now I must go tell Aldo the good news."

Selina grimaced. "And he will not enjoy your news above half, I'll warrant." She got up to see Gemma to the door.

No sooner were the girls out of the room than Daisy said to Flavian, "I do not approve of this—any of it—in the least."

"What?" Flavian looked surprised. "What is it that does not meet with your approval?"

"It is not right to exploit Selina in this way just because she is beautiful. What would you do if she looked like a mudhen?"

"I should expect her to seek work and find it," he said emphatically. "Both she and we are fortunate that she does not in the least resemble a mudhen. As for exploiting her, you agreed with me that her becoming Prinny's mistress would be the best thing for her. Unless memory fails me, you were the one who thought of it in the first place."

"Memory fails you," Daisy said. "I neither thought of it nor approved when you thought of it. I have tried to keep quiet about it, not wanting to disturb Selina any more than she is already, but I want you to know right now, Flavian, that I don't like it at all, and I think what Selina already has suffered is the outside of enough."

"Be easy, me gel. When Selina herself is willing, even

eager for the adventure, I see no reason for you to object."

"I object to my niece becoming an adventuress . . . or worse."

"Shh!" Flavian warned as Selina came back into the room.

"Selina, dear gel, you are sitting in the lap of the gods," he said. "Never have I seen fortune reverse its course so completely and smile so abundantly on one person."

"And never have I heard so many mixed metaphors in one short speech, Uncle. Could they come from your mixed-up mind?"

"Now look here, you don't have to be impertinent!" he snapped. "You know as well as I that we have been trying to think of a way to get you in Carlton House for days and days, and here suddenly an invitation is dropped right into your lap."

"It was meant for those gods in whose lap I was sitting," she said. "It was never meant for me—not from Aldo Barelli."

"You are simply going to have to forget your hard feelings toward him," Flavian advised. "Think of him as a means to an end. Maybe he caused you a bit of bad luck, but now through him your luck is changing. Try to see it that way."

"Would that I didn't have to see it at all," Selina said softly. "Since you have an answer to everything, perhaps you can tell me what I shall wear to Carlton House."

"I think you will need a new gown," Daisy said, resigned to the fact that she could do nothing to change Flavian's mnid. "Perhaps we can get the same *modiste* who made the . . ."

"We can ill afford any new gown, certainly not one

108

made by that *modiste* of the *haut ton*." Flavian said. "She just had a new gown made and she can most certainly wear it. After all, Prinny has never laid eyes upon it; it will be new to him."

Secretly, Flavian would have liked nothing better than to tell Selina she could have any number of new gowns, and it riled and frustrated him that he could not afford to pay for even one. He could, of course, go back to the card room, but just thinking about that caused perspiration to break out across his forehead and in the palms of his hands. He panicked at the mere thought of playing again so soon.

"I know I cannot have a new dress now," Selina said, obviously trying to soothe Flavian, and this made him all the more frustrated, "but I will not wear the water-green silk again. I have worn it twice, and I would be hard put to tell which occasion was worse than the other."

"Surely you are not superstitious about a dress, Selina," Daisy said.

"No, but it has unpleasant associations for me," Selina said.

Flavian knew that his own failures and shortcomings were making him unnecessarily gruff, but he could not stop himself from saying, "You had better forget about such drivel as that, me gel. There is only one thing you should have on your mind right now: you must start at once to learn how to be a courtesan."

Eleven

Every day that passed during the week before the Carlton House squeeze filled Selina with more and more dread, and by the time the day of the event arrived she could not have said which she dreaded more: going to Carlton House with Aldo Barelli, or having to flirt with the Prince once she was there.

However, looking through her wardrobe and trying to decide what to wear filled her with as much despondency as she could handle at one time, so while she was dressing she tried not to think of *what* it was she was dressing for . . . or *whom*. Even though Daisy and Flavian had both been insistent that she wear the water-green silk, she was determined she would not. She finally won her point by reminding them that Gemma had been present both times she had worn the gown and "she will think I have nothing else."

At the last minute, she had chosen a yellow sarsnet with glittering golden spangles, a diaphanous yellow shawl, and gold satin Denmark sandals, a lovely ensemble, albeit not in the latest fashion.

When she went downstairs to await the arrival of Gemma and her uncle, Flavian stood up, a smile slowly spreading across his face. "Whooooeee!" he gloated, "I'll wager Prinny never clapped his eyes on anything like you."

"You look . . . quite nice," Daisy said, a slight note of sadness in her voice. Though he had talked himself hoarse, Flavian still had not managed to convince Daisy that what Selina was about to do was in the best interests of all of them. Finally, he had ended his argument by saying, "It may never happen the way we are planning it. Lately nothing does. Just suppose Selina meets a handsome marquess or duke or viscount, or even an untitled gentleman of quality who takes a fancy to her and decides to make her his wife. Then she will not have to worry about pleasing the Regent. It could happen that way, you know."

"I pray that it does," Daisy said fervently.

"Anything could happen at Carlton House," Flavian added.

"That is what I have heard," Daisy said, her worried expression deepening.

Now, feeling triumphant for the first time since he lost at cards, he said to Selina, "Perhaps you had better practice your curtsy. It would be nothing short of the end of the world if you were to fall over backward or appear clumsy when you are presented to the Prince."

"It would at least call attention to myself, and that is what you want, is it not?" Selina retorted. Nevertheless, she dropped a deep curtsy.

"Perfect!" Flavian said. "Ah yes, our luck is changing now. I can feel it in my bones."

So absorbed were they in their own thoughts that all three of them started as the door knocker sounded the arrival of Gemma and Aldo. Selina heaved a deep sigh, Daisy stared down at her hands in her lap as though she had suddenly grown an alien set of appendages, and it was only Flavian who beamed (as though returning Fortune's smile) as he went to the door.

Selina heard him greeting the guests, heard Gemma return the greeting and then heard the deep voice of Aldo Barelli bidding Flavian a good evening and saying that he was pleased to meet Selina's uncle. And then the three of them were in the drawing room and Selina was forced to look up and smile, though when her eyes met Aldo's she felt more like shivering. Although he was smiling, his eyes seemed to be coldly appraising her as though he was about to paint her and was wondering how to begin on such a hopeless subject.

After being introduced to Daisy, he turned back to Selina and said, "Good evening, Miss Bryand. I am delighted you decided to accompany Gemma and me tonight. You are, as usual, looking exquisite."

"I appreciate the invitation," she said stiffly, ignoring the compliment. "I have never seen the interior of Carlton House and I am looking forward to it." Looking forward to it with more apprehension than I have ever had before, she thought.

"It is going to be such a *lark*!" Gemma cried, her eyes alive with the prospects of such a tantalizingly impressive evening. "I only hope I can refrain from giggling like a schoolgirl when I meet Prinny."

"Do, and I shall leave you at home next time," her uncle warned sternly.

"What if I should forget and say something like 'It is a

112

pleasure to meet you, Your Fatness?'" Gemma began, giggling prematurely.

Aldo gave her a withering look and she stopped instantly.

"Oh, Aldo, you know I wouldn't," she said, "but, Selina, you must promise not to look at me when we are presented or I know I shall go into paroxysms of laughter and we shall both disgrace Aldo."

"I hardly think I shall find the Prince that amusing," Selina said, thinking that, for her, the evening would be anything but a laughing matter. She wondered what Gemma—and her uncle, for that matter—would think if they knew her real reason for going.

"Oh, well," Gemma's attitude turned to one of mock sadness, "there will be so many people packed into the rooms that we may not even get a glimpse of Prinny."

Aldo bowed to the Curtises, he and Gemma said their good-nights and the three of them started out, but Flavian pulled Selina back and whispered to her, "If no opportunity to meet the Prince arises, you must make one, for you will not have another, or better, chance than this."

When Selina merely gave him a long look instead of answering, he added, "Remember, it is getting to be a matter of grave concern. The very roof over our heads depends upon what happens tonight."

"You know I will do what I can, Uncle," she said. "You may depend upon it."

"And another thing, you could be a little nicer to Mr. Barelli. Remember, he *is* a man of substance and a famous artist, and it was our good fortune that he consented to take you tonight."

Without answering, Selina went out the door to catch

up with Gemma and Aldo. It was not part of her bargain with Flavian that she put herself out to be nice to the atrocious Aldo. As far as she was concerned, she would call a truce just for tonight; tomorrow she would go back to detesting him as much as ever—probably more, because he was sure to do something to irritate, if not outrage, her tonight. So far tonight, he had not done one thing right, according to her way of looking at it. She did not like the way he looked at her, the way he spoke to her and, she thought, it was heaven's own miracle that she could not know what he thought of her for she was sure *that* would undoubtedly make her fly up into the boughs.

She was thankful that she did not have to make conversation with him in the carriage. The truth was that Gemma, wild-eyed with excitement, talked incessantly, even to the point of repeating herself several times.

"Oh, Selina, isn't this the grandest occasion you can *imagine*? I never in my wildest *dreams* expected to be invited to a party at Carlton House! It is just . . ."

Selina stopped listening, realizing that she would not be called upon for answers. It would not be unlike Aldo, she thought, to remind Gemma that *she* had not been the one to receive the invitation. But, sitting opposite the two girls in the carriage, he held his tongue. Even in the darkness Selina could tell that he was staring at her moodily, and his silence seemed to have a brooding quality to it.

When they arrived at Carlton House, Selina heaved a deep sigh which sounded not unlike a sob. She did not try to analyze her feelings now; indeed, she thought she probably never would again. It was better not to concentrate on misery, better to remain numb, if possible.

Carlton House, the two-storied mansion which had

been called England's Versailles, was awesome—not so much, Selina decided, because of its appearance, but because of what awaited her inside.

It had taken three architects to achieve, ultimately, what the Prince wanted for his residence. As Aldo helped Selina from the carriage, bowing to her formally, she stared at the house, as unmindful of Aldo's gallantry as to Gemma's running commentary on everything she saw. Words such as "elegant" and "magnificent" were used over and over, but Selina thought the word she would have chosen, were she going to comment, was "ostentatious." There seemed to be too much of everything, including splendor and grandeur.

From the entrance hall to the long reception room and even in the ballroom were works of art, Prinny's treasures, which stunned both the mind and the imagination. Selina was sure that after she left, the entire palace would remain in her memory as a confusion of stained glass, ostrich plumes adorning a canopy of helmets, carved pillars, mirrored walls, gold and silver candlesticks, flowing antique draperies, and porphyry columns with Etruscan griffins.

In the throne room, Gemma whispered, "This room *looks* like Prinny, big and overdone."

"Have you ever seen him?" Selina asked.

"Only from a distance, but Aldo has been here before."

Aldo, who was showing them through the famous residence, said on finishing the tour, "Now let us return to the reception room before the squeeze begins and we won't be able to push our way from one room to another."

"You know," Gemma said confidentially, as though wishing to educate Selina, "this place is as famous for its wild parties as for its art treasure. I do hope it will turn into a wild affair tonight, don't you?"

"Where is the Prince?" Selina asked, inquiring about the thing that was uppermost in her mind.

"He likes to wait until all the guests are assembled and then make an appearance to show off his raiment," Aldo said.

At this, Selina looked around her to see how the guests were attired. Until now, her mind had been in so much turmoil that she had not thought of the matter of dress at all. If the dress at Almack's had astounded her by its finery, this all but blinded her and left her mute. Never had she beheld such glitter, in men as well as women. It appeared that only three materials existed, silk, satin and velvet, and every color and combinations of color were used. In addition to the matter of dress, Selina was equally astonished at the jewels. She had not realized there was so much jewelry in all of England. It would seem that every woman present—herself excepted—owned at least a portion of the crown jewels.

As they reached the large reception room, a servant approached Aldo and said, "Mr. Barelli? His Highness would like to see you in his rooms. Will you come with me." The last was not a question but a command.

Without a word, Aldo followed the man from the room, and in spite of her strong feeling against him, Selina felt a bit lost when he left them. "What shall we do if someone asks us why we are here?" she asked Gemma.

"Selina, you have been all about in your head ever since that dreadful business at Almack's," Gemma told her crisply. "No one is going to ask us why we are here. Anyway, we are here because we are *invited*. Now will you please loosen up some and begin to enjoy yourself?

You act as though you are at an execution instead of a party."

Selina smiled weakly, recognizing the truth of Gemma's words. "I shall try," she promised and then, looking across the wide room, she cried out, "Oh!"

"What is it?" Gemma asked, alarmed. "Are you ill?"

"No, I see someone I know." Even as she said it, Auberon Baldwin looked at her, nodded, and then, surprisingly, started across the room toward her.

"Good evening, Miss Bryand." He bowed to her then looked at Gemma both appraisingly and approvingly. Selina made the introductions, thinking that this was the reason Baldwin had crossed the room—not to see her, as she had hoped, but to meet Gemma.

"Oh, you are the one we saw the day we were walking in the park," Gemma said, artlessly adding, "You were with a girl with red hair."

Baldwin smiled, acknowledging her excellent memory, and Selina felt a small surge of jealousy. Then she chided herself; it was foolish for her to feel anything where Auberon Baldwin was concerned, especially jealousy. He had seen her at her worst—the night she had been asked to leave Almack's—therefore not even seeing her at her best could impress him now.

But what was he saying? He was no longer talking to Gemma but to her. She had been a world away when she should have been listening to him.

"I beg your pardon, but there is the hum of so many voices I did not hear you," she said.

"I asked if you would do me the honor of standing up with me for a waltz before the ballroom becomes so crowded that we can do little more than face each other and stare," he said.

Selina looked at Gemma. More than anything in the world she wanted to waltz with Auberon Baldwin, but she could not be so impolite as to leave Gemma alone among this press of strangers. However, Gemma said instantly, "Oh, do, Selina. You waltz like an angel. Perry and I watched you that night at . . ." She broke off, her face reddening.

"I watched her too," Baldwin said, "and regretted that I was not her partner."

"Yes, but . . ." Selina was about to say that perhaps they could go to the ballroom later when Gemma spotted someone she knew and abruptly left them.

Selina and her escort, who, she thought, looked even handsomer than he had the night at Almack's (and better turned out also) went to the ballroom. He wore a midnight blue waistcoat, exquisitely fitted, and matching satin breeches with white silk stockings.

"You left Almack's so hurriedly that I did not get a chance to ask you to stand up with me for the waltz," he said.

She wondered if he was being sarcastic, and his audacity in bringing up that ill-fated night shocked her. Surely he could not be such a cad as to embarrass her intentionally. She had assumed that by seeing her here in Carlton House, he thought her being asked to leave Almack's surely had been a mistake. And that gave her an idea which she expounded upon at once.

"I left Almack's as quickly as possible because I was so furious at the Lady Patronesses that I was afraid I might forget myself and say something really horrid, especially to the one who made the mistake."

"Mistake?"

"Did you know what was going on?" she asked, hoping

that she had enough acting ability to get her through the explanation without arousing either his suspicion or his contempt. "It was a case of mistaken identity. There is a girl who apparently resembles me closely, and she has been to Almack's several times without a voucher. Since I am comparatively new in town, they thought I was she and asked me to leave."

"Why did you not explain the mix-up instead of leaving?" he asked.

"Because, as I said, I was furious about the mistake, as well as about being the center of such a dreadful scene. I decided it would be better to leave and do the explaining at a more propitious time."

"Then I may hope to see you at Almack's again soon," he said.

"Of course."

"Possibly next Wednesday night," he persisted.

"No, I'm afraid not then. I have another party for that night."

"Really? I thought hostesses would allow themselves to be shot at sunrise before they would schedule anything that would conflict with the Wednesday night ball at Almack's."

Selina realized that she had, out of ignorance, made a bad tactical error. She tried to cover. "It is a bon voyage affair for friends who are leaving for the Continent the next day."

"I see."

She wondered just what he saw and was afraid to probe too deeply for fear of what she might see. Her worse fears seemed to be confirmed as they began waltzing and he said, "I cannot believe that there is another girl anywhere, certainly not in London, who resembles you."

119

She almost stumbled and fell as she stopped dead still, a look of fierceness on her face. "Sir, are you inferring that I am a liar?"

He smiled ingratiatingly. "My dear Miss Bryand, I am saying that nowhere under the sun could there be anyone so beautiful."

Mollified, she allowed his arm again to encircle her waist and they continued dancing, this time omitting any conversation whatever.

Later, he took her back to the reception room to look for Gemma and they saw her standing with Aldo who had returned from his interview with the Prince. Before Baldwin could be introduced, he bowed to Selina and made his way through the now thronged room, disappearing among a sea of faces and closely pressed bodies.

Selina was keenly disappointed, not only that he had made no arrangements to see her at any time in the future, but also that he had not even asked if she would stand up with him again before the evening was over. It was obvious that he was not interested in continuing any acquaintance with her, only in amusing himself momentarily by arousing her pique.

Depressed, she turned to Aldo, another man with whom she could never establish any sort of easy, comfortable friendship in spite of her close friendship with Gemma. Aldo, with his superior manner, was likely to be even ruder than Auberon Baldwin with his pointed questions.

"I trust you enjoyed your visit with the Prince," she said.

"It was not exactly a social visit," Aldo replied. "He asked me to do a portrait of him and I, of course, accepted the honor."

"I suppose you could do nothing else," she said. "It must be like a command performance."

Ignoring that remark, Aldo said, "He will sit for me for a while tomorrow. I will not be able to get him to pose for very long at a time, I expect."

Selina, becoming more and more uncomfortable as Carlton House seemed as though it would burst at the seams with people, asked, "Is the Prince not coming to his own party?"

No sooner had she spoken than a hush fell over the room and His Majesty George, Prince of Wales, Regent of the Realm, stood in the doorway, resplendent in a dark red velvet coat, bone-colored breeches of gleaming satin, and the most intricately tied neckcloth Selina had ever seen. He was elegantly attired, regal looking, had a fairly genial expression on his face and, with it all, was hideously fat and ugly. It was no wonder, Selina thought, that he was sensitive about his appearance. He had a lot to be sensitive about. It was the first time she had ever seen him and she was willing to concede that everything she had ever heard about him was true, even to the slack jaw which gave him a rather lascivious expression.

She stared at him as he accepted the greetings and approbation of those present. One thought was in her mind and one only: she knew, looking at him, that she would never be able to force herself to go through with Flavian's plan.

And yet that thought had no sooner formed in her mind than she knew that she *must* go through with it. She had no alternative.

She continued to stare at him, trying to find some redeeming quality about him, something that would make him seem less repulsive to her. He was in his fifties, looked much older, but dressed much younger. She had heard that he had a great deal of charm and could be quite likeable when the spirit moved him to be, but the thought of getting close enough to him to find out if the rumor were true repelled her. She watched how he moved about the room with heavy self-consciousness and the thought struck her that if she looked like that, she would be self-conscious, too.

So, with that bit of pity for him, she turned to Aldo and said, "Would you be so good as to present me to the Regent?"

Aldo's surprise was obvious by the expression on his face, nevertheless he took her arm and led her through the crush to where the Prince was conversing with a member of parliament and the M. P.'s obese, overly bejewelled wife.

Twelve

The Prince finished his conversation and then turned his attention to Aldo who presented Selina.

"Your niece?" asked the Regent.

Aldo told him that his niece was at this moment in the ballroom for the quadrille and that Selina was a friend.

So absorbed was Selina in observing the Regent close by that she almost forgot her manners. Hastily she dropped a curtsy, thinking as she did that the Prince appeared even fatter than he had from across the room. She murmured "Your Highness," then dared to look up into his face to see what impression she had made.

He nodded, acknowledging her existence, then turned immediately to Aldo. "You will not forget our appointment tomorrow," he said.

"No, Your Highness. I shall be here at the appointed hour," Aldo assured him, and Selina found it passing strange that the Prince Regent should be afraid one of his subjects, albeit a foreign one, would forget an appointment. Or, she thought, perhaps it was all he could think of to say at the moment.

One thing, however, was very clear to her: she had made no impression on him whatsoever. He was now chatting with Aldo, apparently continuing a conversation they had started when Aldo had gone to the royal rooms. What should I do, she wondered, to make him know I am here?

She could think of several negative ways (say to him, "I am enjoying your party, Your Fatness," or, "Did anyone ever tell you that you dress like a man thirty years your junior, Rolly-Polly Regent?") but no positive ways. Besides, she was not supposed to address him again until she was addressed by him. But if she waited for that, she would hear the final bugle of Judgment Day first.

"Your Highness, may I say that Carlton House is every bit as lovely as I had been led to believe?" she interjected into Aldo's conversation, causing Aldo to give her one of his strange, unreadable looks. She went on, anyway. "Your collection of art is truly remarkable, and generations to come will still be praising your good taste."

The slight frown which had appeared on the Regent's face when she began, gradually cleared, and by the time she had finished that little speech, he was beaming. "I congratulate you on *your* good taste, Madam." Which was a left-handed way of complimenting himself. He gave her the slightest bow.

Her small triumph was short-lived, however, for the Prince immediately turned his back on her and Aldo and began talking to someone behind them.

There was nothing else she could do or say now to get his attention—not without creating a scene equal to or worse than the one at Almack's, and she had already

124

vowed that never again would she become a public spectacle, no matter what the circumstances.

She had to accept the fact that Prinny was totally uninterested in her. Flavian had been wrong in his suppositions that one look at her would bring the Regent to his knees begging for her favors. The Regent had not even cared to prolong a first look, let alone take a second one.

She was forced to admit to herself that she was a failure as a woman. Not only was she not desired as a wife, but it was obvious that she was not even wanted as a mistress.

Her emotions about her sovereign were somewhat mixed. On the one hand, she had been fearful of what would happen should he be attracted to her; on the other, she felt insulted because of his complete lack of interest.

"Yes, what is it?" she said impatiently to Aldo, realizing that he had said something to her.

"Since you commented upon the works of art, I would like to show you some of the *real* ones here. What you have seen so far is not the best of what is on show. Come."

That "come" could have been no more a royal command if Prinny himself had uttered it, and she resented it. She longed to tell Aldo she had no desire to follow him on another tour of Carlton House; indeed, all she wanted now was to go home and forget this third evening of absolute frustration and failure.

With a frown on her face that could easily turn into the darkest scowl, she left the reception room with Aldo, went past the ballroom where she caught a glimpse of Gemma dancing with Auberon Baldwin (and without realizing what she was doing, she stopped dead still and stared), and on to a long gallery which was filled from one end to the other with paintings and works of sculpture. This gallery, apparently, contained what Aldo considered the "real" art in Prinny's collection.

"Now you may feast your eyes," he said. He took her arm and guided her down the length of the gallery, telling her the artist and a little about the paintings, pointing out sculpture by men of prominence of men of prominence. She did not listen. She looked and appeared to be interested, but her mind was on Gemma dancing in the arms of Auberon Baldwin and on what she would say to Flavian when she returned home. Two rebuffs in one evening were not to be borne. How could she face him and admit a third evening of failure on all counts? After all Flavian and Daisy had done for her these past years, she wanted to be able to repay them in some way, and now there was no way left to her. There was nothing she could do but go home, admit her failure, and be forever a burden on them. She knew Flavian would never consent to her seeking any kind of menial work; he was much too high-minded to have anyone from his household doing the work of a servant. And she did not have enough formal education to be a governess . . .

"I think you know the artist here," Aldo was saying.

She could, she thought, be a paid companion to some wealthy old woman, but from what she had seen of the life of "companions" and the abuse that was heaped upon them by their usually ill-tempered principals, she would rather be a scullery maid.

"You do not seem to be with me," Aldo said in a not unkindly tone. "Where is your mind, Selina?"

His calling her by her given name for the first time brought her out of her thoughts. "I am sorry," she apologized halfheartedly. "What were you saying?"

"I said I think you know the artist here."

She looked at the painting they were standing in front of and glanced hastily at the signature in the lower right hand corner. *A. Barelli.*

The painting was of a lake with a village on one shore and mountains in the background. The scene itself was unremarkable, but the colors were extraordinary—so deep and rich that they made the painting overshadow those on either side of it. It was unlike anything she had ever seen before.

"It is lovely," she said, "truly lovely. Is it a real place or did it come from your imagination?"

"It is the village where I was born, on a lake north of Venice."

"But I thought you came from Rome—or near there."

"I went to Rome to live when I finished my schooling, after I had achieved some notoriety as an artist."

There was no question about his talent as an artist, she thought, but his talent for social intercourse left much to be desired. It had occurred to her just then that he had brought her here, not to expound on the Prince's art and educate her tastes, but to show her his own painting in the Carlton House gallery. He was trying to impress her, but she could not imagine why. It seemed out of character that he would want to, especially in view of his past behavior toward her.

As she turned away from his painting, he said, "I suppose the Prince will hang the portrait I do of him in here also."

She knew then that he was not trying to impress her, merely assert his superiority in yet another way. He was still the same abominable, atrocious Aldo, he of the rag-manners and ramshackle behavior.

"I would like to go back to the ballroom," she said, wanting to see what progress Gemma was making with Auberon Baldwin—though why she wanted to torture herself in this way she could not imagine.

Although there were a few people wandering through the gallery, it was like a deserted island compared to the squeeze that greeted them as soon as they stepped through the door. It was impossible, even in the ballroom, to find anyone; one moved with the crowd, to do otherwise would be insanity.

Then Selina spotted Gemma standing at the door of the ballroom with a young man she had never seen before. It was not Auberon Baldwin, she thought thankfully. She was about to desert Aldo and go to Gemma when someone touched her arm. She whirled around and faced the real object of her search, Auberon himself.

"Oh!" she exclaimed, unable to hide her delight, and also unhappy with herself for being so transparent. "I thought you were among those dancing."

"I was," he said. "I had a dance with Miss Moraldo and then I went looking for you. You seemed to have vanished from the face of the earth—from Carlton House, at least."

"I was looking at the treasures in the gallery with Mr. Barelli," she told him. She was about to introduce the two men when Auberon said, "Would you do me the honor of going in to supper with me? You know, you promised I could be your supper escort at Almack's, and then you left before you kept your promise."

She tried not to show how uncomfortable any talk of that ill-fated night made her, but she did not have to reply at once for Auberon continued, "It will be much better here—the food, I mean—for at Almack's there is only a table of light refreshments while you can count on Prinny for a real repast."

"I should be delighted to go with you," she said, and turning, still ready to make the introductions, she was stopped instantly by the black look on Aldo's face. Never had she seen such an expression of anger and disapproval. It would be a draw, she thought, as to which of us detests the other more.

With that, she forgot about the introductions, put her hand on Auberon's arm and said, "I am famished. Could we go now?"

She did not glance back at Aldo as they left the ball-room, but she knew that he was glaring at her, and if looks could burn she would have been scorched beyond recognition.

The banquet hall, to which Auberon escorted her, looked almost as festive as Selina felt. She could hardly take in the candelabra, the tapestries, the gold and silver flatware and gold and silver plates for her feeling of tri-umph at having again been paid attention by Auberon. There were three tables which extended the length of the room, and people were filing in now, ready to behold whatever delicacies the Regent's cooks had prepared. But Selina cared not whether they were fed the world's most delectable cuisine or cold porridge, so happy was she to find that she had been mistaken about Auberon. Obvi-ously, she had *not* failed there or he would not have asked her to be his supper partner. She also must have been wrong about his interest in Gemma or it would have been Gemma, not Selina, who was now being seated beside him by one of the liveried footmen serving in the banquet hall.

The meal itself consisted of every imaginable kind of

food and drink. There was every wine that Selina had ever heard of, in addition to some she had not. There were roast lamb and roast beef, ham and lobster and quail, at least a dozen vegetables and as many fruits and cheeses, followed by cakes and crèmes.

Selina did not begin to eat when food was placed in front of her, thinking that the guests surely should wait for the host to come in, but she noticed that others up and down the table were half through with their supper.

"Isn't the Prince going to join his guests?" she asked.

"I should doubt it," Auberon told her. "It is my understanding that he eats when he has a few close friends in, but that when it is a squeeze, like tonight, he prefers to mingle with the guests who are still looking over Carlton House. I have heard he never tires of showing off the palace and what he has done to it, along with his art treasures, of course."

Or it could be, Selina thought, that as fat as he is, he is a bit sensitive about eating before so many people.

Somehow, that thought made him a little more human in her estimation. The Regent did not like to be ridiculed or embarrassed any more than the lowliest of his subjects did.

The hum of voices in the room kept conversation between her and Auberon at a minimum, but they did manage to gaze at each other between courses and smile contentedly, and she had a feeling that this time he would not let her go without making plans to see her again in the future.

She was wrong, however, for he was not given a chance to say more than good-night to her when the supper was finished. Aldo, who with Gemma was eating near the head of the next table, suddenly was standing behind Selina's chair saying to her, "I hope you have finished, Miss Bryand, for we must be going."

Selina was too surprised to say anything. She could only hope that Auberon would tell her to send Aldo on his way so that he could take her home himself. Auberon did no such thing, though. He merely stood up in anticipation of her standing, and when she did, he bade her good-night, thanked her for being his supper partner, and said he hoped to see her again sometime.

"Yes, I hope so, too," she said, trying not to let either him or Aldo see how disturbed she was at having to leave.

She did not say another word, either to Aldo or Gemma, not even when they were in the carriage leaving the Carlton House gaiety. It was Gemma who voiced her anger at being taken away so early.

"Aldo, you are a *monster* of the first magnitude for taking us away while everybody else is still having such a good time. What in the *world* can you be thinking about? Have you gone apoplectic?"

Aldo gave a little laugh which sounded to Selina much more like a growl.

"It is not well to wear out your welcome, particularly the first time you are a guest," he said.

"That doesn't make a particle of sense and you know it!" Gemma cried. "That was not *your* first visit to Carlton House and, besides, there are still so many people that Prinny won't know who is there and who is not."

"Ah, but don't you see? It is when he looks around and *misses* you that you can know you are the *crème de la crème* of the polite world."

"You are still a monster and I would call you something worse, only I can't think of anything bad enough,"

131

Gemma pouted. "So from now on I don't think I will say anything at all to you. I will talk only to Selina."

But she was too busy nursing her anger at Aldo to converse with Selina, and so the ride to Half Moon Street continued in silence.

When the carriage stopped, Aldo helped Selina out and escorted her to the door. Selina was about to thank him for including her in the invitation, but when he bowed to her formally and curtly bid her good-night, she merely murmured good-night between clenched teeth, shrugged with indifference and went into the house.

What a rotten evening it had turned out to be after all. She had had to put up with the atrocious Aldo, and the Prince Regent had been most decidedly unimpressed by her.

No—she amended the earlier thought—the evening had not been a *complete* failure. She had been inside Carlton House, something achieved only by a few privileged people and close friends of the Regent, and she had become better acquainted with Auberon Baldwin. But it did gall her no end to think that both had been accomplished through Aldo Barelli.

Thirteen

Daisy had already retired, but Favian met Selina at the door, questions pouring from him like water from a pitcher. "Did you meet Prinny? What was Carlton House like? Is it gaudy? When is the Prince going to see you again? Has he invited you to a smaller, more intimate party? What did you think of him?"

Selina held up both hands. "Please, Uncle, I can only answer one question at a time, and, truthfully, I am too tired to answer even one tonight. Can we not talk tomorrow?" She thought it significant that the last question he asked was whether she had liked the Regent; it would signify that he asked his questions in the order of diminishing importance.

"By tomorrow you may have forgotten some of the details, and I want to hear everything. I *must* hear everything," he said.

It would do no good to tell him that, all in all, the evening had not been a success and that she was not only too

133

tired but also too depressed to talk about it. That would only cause him to be even more dejected about their future. It would be better to let him get a good night's sleep and then tell him the details in the morning. Somehow everything always seemed worse at night.

"Yes, I met the Regent," she said. "Carlton House is very much as people say it is: elegant in an overblown sort of way, although there were so many people milling about that it was hard to see a great deal of it."

"What did you think of Prinny?"

"He, also, is very much as everyone says he is: fat."

"Now, Selina!"

"Well, he is."

"And what did he think of you?"

She could have brought the inquisition to a halt by answering, "He didn't think of me at all." Instead, she said, "He said I have good taste."

Flavian beamed with satisfaction. "I knew we had only to let him see you and everything else would work itself out. When will you see him again?"

"I am not sure." That was as close to a lie as she had come yet, and she did not want to get any closer. "Please, Uncle, I am simply too fatigued to talk any more. I will tell you all about it tomorrow."

Realizing that he would get no more from her tonight, he reluctantly said good-night. She went upstairs to her bedchamber, glad to be by herself, finally. Solitude was what she needed right now, and a great deal of it.

The next morning Selina still could not bring herself to tell Flavian the whole story of the night at Carlton House. She could not bear to see that look of disappointment come into his face, the hopelessness return to his eyes.

What she hoped was that she would hear from Auberon Baldwin, and then she could tell Flavian that the night at Prinny's party had not gone entirely as they had planned, but that all was not lost. If Auberon showed an interest, and it seemed likely he would, Flavian could take heart again.

However, when two days went by and there was no word from Auberon, Selina again became very despondent. She spent much time brooding in her bedchamber. It occurred to her that even if Auberon began to shower attention upon her, he would stop as soon as he found out her circumstances. It was not likely that a young man who was welcome at Almack's and invited to Carlton House would consider an alliance of any kind with a girl who was without dowry, even without a family name of consequence. That opinion was more than confirmed when she looked up the name Baldwin in a book of the peerage, Flavian's only contribution to the scant library, and found that Auberon was the son of Lord Hanley Baldwin, M.P.

By the third day when there were no callers or messages for Selina, it entered Flavian's mind that had Prinny been as entranced with Selina as he, Flavian, had anticipated, there would have been royal messengers at the door and maybe even the royal coach in front of the door waiting to take Selina back to Carlton House. He became even more despondent than Selina.

Daisy remarked on it to Selina. "I believe Flavian has caught your malady."

"What malady, Aunt?"

"The one known as Long Face. He has been in the depths all day, and I can find no reason for it. It cannot be our financial affairs, for he has never let money—nor lack of it—bother him much."

Selina, wondering if Daisy would not have an even worse case of Long Face than Flavian if she knew about Flavian's dwindling inheritance, tried to speak in a cheerful tone when she said, "He is probably worried about me, and the fact that the Regent was not taken with me."

"To me that is more cause for relief than worry," Daisy said. "I was never in favor of that bit of scheming, in the first place."

"Uncle seems to think it is the only way to secure our future."

"I might agree with him if there were a pressing need to get our hands on money immediately, but there is certainly no reason to rush you into an unsavory liaison that does not please you," Daisy said.

All of which made Selina want to burst into tears. Knowing more about the Curtis financial affairs than Daisy was an extra burden for her.

"Don't worry about me, Aunt. I shall be all right—with or without the Prince," was all she could think of to say.

It was Gemma who brought hope into the house that afternoon, although at the time, after hearing what Gemma had to say, Selina was more angry than hopeful.

Gemma seated herself in the drawing room in the chair which automatically was thought of as Flavian's, and she paused dramatically before saying anything. Flavian and Daisy, after speaking to Gemma, had withdrawn to the bookroom so the girls could feel more free in chatting, however Selina was sure that their ears, Flavian's at least, would be turned toward the drawing room for Gemma had greeted her with, "I have the *most* astonishing news for you," then she clapped her hands over her mouth, mumbling between her fingers something about being careful, because Selina was supposed to hear the news later, not now.

"What is the news?" Selina asked as soon as they were alone.

"You will find out in good time," Gemma said maddeningly. "First, I have an invitation for you."

Selina groaned, remembering all too well Gemma's invitations in the recent past and where they had led.

"You will be excited about this one, I promise you," Gemma assured her. "It is the best possible surprise, and so unexpected."

"Well, what is it?" Selina asked, beginning to feel a modicum of excitement in spite of herself.

"Aldo wants me to bring you back with me to have dinner with us."

Selina's rising hopes fell so flat that she was sure there must have been an attending thud. She looked at Gemma as though the girl's last shred of sense had gone on leave.

"Really, Selina, this is no jest," Gemma insisted. "Aldo told me to come for you and not to return without you."

The gall of that man! Selina thought. The unmitigated gall! "Sorry," she said stiffly. "I never accept last-minute or spur-of-the-moment invitations."

"But you must!" Gemma insisted. "Actually, it is more a command performance than an invitation."

This angered Selina so much that she could hardly speak. Command performance indeed! When she felt she could keep her temper at least partially under control, she said, "I find it worse than Mr. Barelli's usual rag-manners, his issuing *any* command in my direction. I am not a servant to whom he can give orders—not yet, anyway." She added the latter under her breath.

"Selina . . ."

"And if that is your idea of exciting news, Gemma, I am afraid you need to look up the definition of excitement."

"Listen, Selina! Will you just listen for a minute?" Gemma looked as though she was not sure whether she should laugh or cry. "The invitation for dinner is not the news. I would tell you the news right now but Aldo made me promise I wouldn't. He wants to tell you himself—and I can't say that I blame him, it is such astonishingly *good* news. So you see, you simply *have* to go back with me in order to find out what the news is."

Selina was about to refuse again, but the imploring look on Gemma's face stopped her. And maybe this time Gemma was not exaggerating in her usual ebullient, overstated way.

"Will you give me a hint as to what the news is?" Selina asked, thinking she could find out if it would be worth tolerating the Atrocious Aldo for an evening.

"I am afraid to," Gemma said, giggling. "I might let the secret out and then Aldo would *murder* me. But I can promise you that it is something that is going to please you. There, that's all I am going to say until after Aldo has told you."

Suddenly, like a brilliant sunrise in a sky dark with thunderheads, it came to Selina what the news was—what it *had* to be. Carlo had called off his wedding and was coming back to London to offer for Selina again.

"All right," she said, this time without the least hesitation in her voice. "I will go with you."

Fourteen

Selina, who was wearing a blue cambric dress when Gemma arrived, did not even bother to change before going to the house on Grosvenor Square. There would be only Aldo and Gemma present, and she had no intention of wasting time and effort on Aldo. Had she been wearing her oldest morning dress she probably would not have changed that either, she thought.

Gemma prattled away in the carriage, but Selina hardly listened to a word she said. Her thoughts were still on the "astonishingly good" news she would hear when they arrived . . . It was time for good news, she thought, time for all the bad events and bad news of the past weeks to be counteracted by something pleasant.

As they went in the grand entry hall, the butler appeared almost magically and announced in magisterial tones that Mr. Barelli would join them shortly in the blue saloon.

Another example of Aldo's bad manners, Selina

thought, resenting the fact that he felt free to keep her waiting. She almost said as much to Gemma, but decided not to, for Gemma had heard her raving on about Aldo many times before, and the girl was in no way responsible for her uncle's behavior. Besides, she had remained amazingly good-humored during Selina's complaints about her adored uncle, and Selina could see no reason to continue those complaints and make Gemma unhappy. Also, if what she suspected was true, she would be a member of the family soon, and Aldo would be *her* uncle as well.

They waited only a few minutes before Aldo appeared, and he was dressed to the nines in a beautifully fitted coat of blue superfine and breeches a few shades lighter. He was smiling as though he had come to greet his dearest friend, and Selina thought she had never seen him looking handsomer or acting with more charm. He bent over her hand, kissed it, and said, "In Italy it is incorrect for a gentleman to kiss the hand of an unmarried woman, but I understand that quaint rule is not always observed here."

Selina was speechless.

"I am glad you found it convenient to return with Gemma," he said—just as though he had not *ordered* that she return with his niece, "for I have something to discuss with you. First, though, we shall have a glass of wine." He pulled the bell cord and the butler appeared instantly. Aldo merely nodded, and the butler left the room. He returned in only a moment with a decanter of wine and three glasses on a silver tray. Selina had no idea what kind of wine it was, but she would have wagered a great deal on its being Italian wine and not French.

Aldo raised his glass and looked at Gemma and then at Selina. "To our lovely guest," he said, "who adorns this room like a work of art of inestimable value."

"Thank you," Selina murmured, still stunned by Aldo's apparent good humor and, for a change, good manners. She was actually beginning to feel like a welcome guest instead of an interloper whom Aldo wished to show to the door at the first possible moment.

"The blue of your dress matches this room exactly," Gemma pointed out. "You look as though you belong here."

Selina blushed and acknowledged the compliment, and in her mind she agreed with Gemma: she did belong here. And if Carlo was really returning, she would be here. This would be her home—after she put Carlo through a short period of wondering whether she would accept him. It would serve him right after what he had put her through. As to how she would get along with Aldo, she was not sure. But if he made a great effort, as he was tonight, she would certainly do her part.

The wine finished, Aldo gave Selina his arm and the three of them went in to dinner. Although the conversation was steady during the soup course and the fish course, nothing of import was said. Mostly, they commented on Carlton House and the Prince, and Selina was somewhat surprised when Aldo asked her, in all seriousness, what she thought of the Prince.

"Why, I'm not sure," she said.

"I am sure," Gemma piped up. "I think he is a fat clown, only he isn't funny, except unintentionally."

"Not a very charitable opinion," Aldo commented.

"I think," Selina said slowly, "that he is like Carlton House, a bit overdone, extreme."

"Extreme in what way?" Aldo looked politely interested.

"In every way," she said. "He dresses too youthfully

for his age, his palace and his parties are too lavish, he is too wild—at least I have heard that he is—and, of course, one only has to look at him to see in what other way he is extreme."

"You mean the leering looks he give the ladies?" Gemma asked.

"I was referring to his obesity," Selina said. "In a way, I feel a bit sorry for him."

"Sorry for him!" Aldo and Gemma exclaimed simultaneously, then Aldo asked, "Why do you feel sorry for him?"

"I am not sure," Selina said, "but there appears to me to be something a little pathetic about him—as though he is trying so hard to attain something, but is not sure what that something is."

"Oh, he knows what he wants, all right," Aldo said, adding in a much lower tone, "and I hope your sympathy does not get you into trouble."

"Why should it?" Selina asked. "I probably shall never see him again—at least not at such close quarters."

The subject was changed abruptly by Aldo as the squab was brought in, and Selina began to wonder if there was a secret to be told or if she had been brought here by Gemma because the girl wanted her closest friend and her uncle to make up their differences and be friends also. She herself fell silent and concentrated on the delicious food. Gemma talked, as usual, but got only monosyllabic answers from Aldo who also seemed to have his mind very much on the spread before him.

After the meat course, fruit and cheese were brought in, followed by Queen's cakes with a creamy sauce. Just as the three of them were finishing the dessert, and Selina was beginning to despair of hearing any news at all, let

142

alone "astonishingly good news," Aldo gave an almost imperceptible nod to Gemma and she immediately excused herself and left the table. She said as she went out, "I don't know why I can't stay. I want to see Selina's face when you tell her."

Aldo said nothing, but as soon as she was out of the room, he turned to Selina.

"You may wonder why I sought out your opinion of the Regent," he said. "You must believe me, I had a very good reason."

Selina, who had expected to hear him say something like, "I have news for you; it appears that Carlo has decided to call off his wedding and return to London," did not quite comprehend this sudden return to the subject of the Prince.

"I am sure you did," she said. "I am sure you have a very good reason for everything you do." No, she told herself, you must not be rude or sarcastic to him when he is obviously trying, for once, to make himself agreeable.

If he detected the sarcasm in her voice, he ignored it. "I went to Carlton House, as arranged, to begin the portrait of the Prince but he did not want to sit for me."

"Oh? And why did he change his mind so quickly? After all, did he not ask *you* rather than your asking him?"

"Instead of sitting for his portrait, he spent the allotted time asking questions about you."

"About *me*? I think you are bamming me, Mr. Barelli."

"Not at all," he said. Then his face took on a rather distasteful expression. "I think he mainly wanted to know just what your relationship to me is. I told him you are a friend of my niece."

"I thought I was supposed to have been a niece also, just for that evening."

"That was not the kind of relationship His Majesty's mind was thinking about, I surmised," Aldo said.

Selina blushed at the words. Then, thinking of what he had said, she became more than a little irritated. The very idea of anyone thinking there was a "relationship" between her and the Atrocious Aldo. It would be almost amusing were the idea not so shocking to her.

"I certainly hope you set him straight on that score," she said, somewhat haughtily.

"You may rest assured that I did so at once." His haughtiness equalled, if not surpassed, her own.

Then slowly it occurred to Selina that Aldo was certainly much younger and handsomer than the Regent with whom she was striving for just such a relationship. But it would be far easier to imagine herself with Prinny than with the insufferable Aldo Barelli.

"To shorten the story, to tell you quite bluntly," Aldo began "the Prince decided that instead of his sitting for me, he would rather that you did. He wants me to postpone his portrait and do one of you first."

Selina was too stunned to do anything but stare uncomprehendingly at her host. Finally, she managed, "But he hardly noticed me, he . . ."

"Oh, he noticed you all right," Aldo said, a trace of bitterness in his voice. "George, Prince of Wales, will be blind, unconscious, or dead the day he does not notice a beautiful woman."

He sounded resentful, she thought, because the Regent wanted him to do her portrait. And the reason was, she was sure, because he had his heart set on painting the future King of England and having his work displayed in some prominent place for all the world to see. Yet, angry as she was with Aldo, she found herself secretly pleased by his unintentional and offhand compliment. He had, in a roundabout way, called her a beautiful woman, and to receive a commendatory word from him was indeed a rare experience.

Then, finally, the import of Aldo's words began to take precedence over her irritation with him and her surprise at the Regent's request. She became more and more elated as she thought that she had not failed after all. The Regent *had* noticed her, and he wanted to see her again . . . at least, he wanted to see her likeness. But surely, he would not let it stop there.

It could mean only one thing: Flavian had been right about Prinny from the beginning.

"When will you begin the portrait?" she asked.

"As soon as possible," Aldo said. "I was not sure you would consent to sit for it. You did refuse me, you know, and that was only a short while ago."

"I was refusing *you*, not the Regent," she said, emphasizing the difference in his request and the Regent's command.

"It is to be done at Carlton House, the sittings, I mean," Aldo said. "The Regent wants to watch the progress of the portrait."

She nodded, knowing full well that that was not all the Regent wanted to watch.

"Are you sure you want to do this?" he asked. "You can refuse if you want to. I assure you, you will not be decapitated or penalized in any way if you had rather not . . ."

"I just told you that one does not refuse a command performance from one's sovereign," she answered tartly.

Aldo glanced at her, a ferocious scowl on his face, but he said nothing. His dark eyes had clouded with that unreadable look which she had come to know well, but under which she still cringed.

Then, as suddenly as it had come, the elation left her as she began to think about posing for Aldo—which would be bad enough, Lord knew—with the licentious Prinny looking on with that sickeningly lustful expression on his face. She wondered if she could go through with it, for there was not the slightest doubt in her mind as to where those "sittings" would lead.

She looked at Aldo again and knew that there was no doubt in his mind either as to the result of the portrait painting sessions. He was bound to know that he was being used as a mere tool by a lewd old man with a desire for a young, comely girl.

She folded her serviette and arose from the table. "I think I should go now," she said. "Will you please inform your coachman?"

"I understand. You want some time alone to think over the . . . er . . . the offer."

"Not at all," she said immediately, not wanting him to know that she was dubious about the venture. "I wish to lose no time in telling my aunt and uncle of the singular honor that has befallen me."

Fifteen

"*Do you want me to build a fire?*" Flavian asked. He and Daisy were sitting in the drawing room, having finished their meager meal of pigeon pie. It was not nearly cold enough for one to need a fire, but Flavian had a restlessness in him that could only be cured by action, and building a fire was the only thing he could think of to do.

Daisy looked up from the book she was pretending to read. "If you want to," she said, "though I do not think it necessary. I believe spring has finally come to stay."

"Deuced strange weather we have been having this year," Flavian said. "And not only the weather . . ." He broke off, afraid he might say too much.

"Flavian, what *is* it?" Daisy laid the book aside.

"What is what?" His face was a picture of innocent incomprehension.

"You know very well what I mean. What is it that is worrying you so? What is it that has had you almost out

147

of your mind for the past fortnight? I am thinking that you are about ready for commitment to Bedlam."

"Now, Daisy, me gel, I might ask you the same question." He tried to laugh, to make light of her worries. "Seems you have been doing your share of the fretting lately."

"Of course I have. Do you think I can go blithely through the days when both you and Selina seem on the verge of insanity? I want you to tell me what is wrong, Flavian, and I want you to tell me right this minute. I am tired to trying to guess and trying to pretend that I think nothing is amiss. Is it money?"

"Certainly not!" Flavian did his best to look appalled at the suggestion that he might be in financial difficulty. "Where did you get such a mush-brained idea?"

"Then what is it?" Daisy was beginning to look and to sound exasperated.

"Nothing that you don't already know about, me gel. Honestly." He stared straight into her eyes, attesting to the truthfulness of his reply. "I admit I have been a trifle concerned about Selina and what will happen to her. I had thought if we could get her established as Prinny's . . . er, as the Prince's love, that we would never have to worry about her again—or ourselves. But it seems I overestimated the Prince's vulnerability to beautiful women. Strange, too, because after all I have heard about him along that line, I thought I had everything figured just right."

Daisy sighed and picked up the book again. She did not want to go any further with this discussion, for Selina's future was the one subject on which she and Flavian constantly disagreed.

At that moment the front door opened and a dazed

148

looking Selina entered the house and came into the drawing room.

"What is the matter?" Daisy cried at once. "What has happened?"

Flavian could not tell by the look of the girl whether something dreadful or something good had happened, but he did know that she had just been a part of some momentous event. She had been to Grosvenor Square to have dinner with Barelli and his niece, and Flavian could not imagine much in the way of excitement taking place at a quiet family dinner, but obviously something had.

"Mr. Barelli had news for me," Selina said, removing her light pelisse. "It seems the Prince wants him to paint my portrait."

"Well, I'll be cooked in oil!" It took a minute or so for this information—and the possible ramifications—to register in Flavian's mind, but when it did his heart began to hop and skip and jump as though it were trying to get out of his body. "Tell!" he cried, unable to get out but that one word.

"Barelli was to do a portrait of the Prince," Selina said, "and when he went to begin, the Prince told him that he wanted to postpone his sittings and have Barelli do a portrait of me, instead."

Flavian's heart stopped its merry peregrinations. "He wants a portrait of you," he said as though this morsel had suddenly become very hard to digest. "Good God, a portrait! Tell me, pray, why he doesn't want *you*?"

"I think he does," Selina said quietly. "I am to sit for the portrait at Carlton House, and I understand the Prince is to be present also to watch Barelli's progress."

"Hallelujah!" Flavian threw his arms up in thanksgiving and celebration. He glanced at Daisy to see how she was taking this miraculous, much-wanted news. Her face was as expressionless as she could make it, he decided.

"Ah, Selina dear, did I not tell you how it would be once His Highness got a glimpse of you?"

"Yes, uncle, you told me," Selina said wearily. She started out of the room. "I believe I shall retire now."

"But, but . . ." He could not believe that she could go to sleep after imparting such a jewel of information. "Would you not like a glass of champagne? I believe there is a bottle here somewhere. We should toast your new status."

"I have no new status—yet." Selina left them staring at each other, Flavian wild-eyed in his happiness, Daisy looking vaguely troubled and yet resigned.

Flavian awoke with a smile on his face the next morning, and it did not take him very long to remember why it was there. His luck had changed for the better—finally! The world had righted itself again, all of that terrible upheaval both within and without him had stopped, and Dame Fortune once again was giving him a radiant smile. Selina would become the Prince's mistress; she would live the rest of her life in luxury—and, just incidentally of course, he and Daisy would have no more worries over money ever again. What a grand joke on the whole world! He, Flavian Curtis, son of a smithy, would be royally (literally!) taken care of for as long as he lived.

He got out of bed hardly remembering how unhappy he had been only recently, thinking that he would never know anything but unending joy in the future. As long as he could be a gentleman (with a gentleman's privileges and a gentleman's leisure) and never have to work at anything, including cards, his life would be the epitome of rhapsodic bliss.

Cards. He had not thought about a card game for a long time, mainly because he had not wanted to think about it. But this morning it was all right to let his mind loose on the subject.

After a few minutes of cogitation, he realized that it had not been his fault that he had lost so ingloriously the last time he played. He had played during that black period when nothing was going right with any part of his life. Now all was well once more, and his confidence, so badly maimed by Lord Hanley Baldwin, was recovering quickly.

He left the house fairly early, looking for a runner to take a message to Lord Baldwin requesting that His Lordship meet him at the same gaming-house where they had met that first time.

This was the day—he could feel it in his bones—that he would win back all he had lost to Lord Baldwin, and then he would destroy his note, and then go on to make a sizeable profit. It occurred to him that not only would Selina need a new wardrobe for her amatory adventures, but he and Daisy also would need to be suitably clad for their presentation to society. After all, when one's niece was a mistress to the Regent, one did not continue to live in obscurity.

Lord Baldwin was already seated at the same table in the small back room where they had played before when Flavian arrived. His Lordship stood up, a jovial smile on his face, his hand extended. "I see you are ready to lose some more money," he greeted Falvian.

Flavian gave him a forced smile, shook his hand, then

sat down opposite him. "I was not sure you would be here."

"I never refuse an invitation to fatten the coffers," Lord Baldwin said. "That is one of my greatest weaknesses."

"I think that we shall find that another of your weaknesses is your game," Flavian said. "I trust you brought my note with you today, for I expect to have the pleasure of tearing it up."

Lord Baldwin chuckled and began dealing the cards. The smile on his face diminished considerably, however, when he looked at his hand.

Flavian's face remained expressionless through the game, even when he was easily victorious. Inside, though, he was a-quiver with excitement. That other time had only been an offday, the first he had ever had in a lifetime of card playing. Now he was back on course, sailing easily toward a port of gold—or a pot of gold. He almost chortled at that thought.

He also took the second game, and he found it a bit disconcerting that the broad smile remained on Lord Baldwin's face. Was the man too idiotish to realize that he was being very soundly beaten? Or was it merely that the loss of a great deal of money did not disturb him?

Flavian smacked his lips. Someday—someday very soon—he himself would be in the position where he could afford to lose vast sums without giving the loss a second thought. But, he amended the thought, when he was in that position, there would be no need for him to play any more.

Oh, deuce take it! He had let his mind wander—just as it had the last time—and Baldwin had taken a game. But it was only one game, while he himself had won two.

In the next game he tried valiantly to keep his mind on

the cards and nothing but the cards. Yet he could not entirely forget how badly the cards, and his luck, had gone before. Just thinking about it made his confidence wane. What if he should lose again? It would be nothing short of tragedy.

He lost again.

"We are two-two," Lord Baldwin said unnecessarily. "Would you like to stop before you get hurt too badly?"

Flavian eyed his opponent without making the scathing comment which came to his mind. What he said was, "If you are afraid to go on, I shall agree to stop."

"Afraid!" His Lordship exploded. "My dear fellow, when it comes to a little game of cards, I do not know the meaning of the word fear. Deal, sir."

Flavian found his opponent's confidence unnerving. Was it possible that Lord Baldwin had a past history at cards similar to his own? It could be that two natural-born winners were playing each other. And, of course, one of the winners would have to become a loser.

Flavian lost the next two games.

"If it is beginning to hurt, we can stop," Lord Baldwin said. "I am not sure about your finances, but . . ." He let the sentence trail off ominously.

His money, or lack of it, was the one thing about which Flavian *was* sure. He had been wagering money he did not have ever since he walked into the gaming-hell.

He thought for several minutes, trying to devise the best way out of his situation. Finally, it came to him that he should play one more game, make the stakes outrageously high—so high that he not only could pay off his losses today but also get back his note—and then quit.

"If you are worried about my paying, I suggest that I offer you something more tangible than my word," he said. He took a piece of paper out of his pocket, wrote upon it, then handed it across the table. "I wish to wager my house on Half Moon Street on this next game, with you putting up money of like value. And I propose we make this the last game."

Lord Baldwin looked at him for a long time as though trying to figure out some quaint personality quirk, then he smiled and nodded in agreement.

Both men were silent as they looked at their cards. Now His Lordship was as expressionless as Flavian and this bothered Flavian a bit. If he wasn't smiling, did that mean he had nothing to smile about or did he simply want Flavian to think he had nothing to smile about?

"Your play, I believe," Lord Baldwin said after waiting a few minutes.

"Oh, sorry." He threw down a card hastily, realizing too late that it was the wrong card.

Lord Baldwin scooped it up, and then the next, and his face became wreathed in smiles again.

Dear Lord, what am I doing? Flavian thought as panic took over both his mind and his game. He was letting the man do something no one else had ever done to him at cards, namely, get him so addled that he was unsure of himself and his game.

One of the natural-born winners would have to become a loser, he thought again, his confidence now completely gone. He must concentrate as he had never concentrated before.

But it was too late.

Lord Baldwin's last card topped his by six points.

Quickly, Flavian picked up the deck and began dealing. "One more," he said, "and then we will quit."

"Have you forgotten? That was our last one."

Flavian was filled with rage and he wanted to give vent to his frustration by punching a hole right in the middle of that loathsome smile. "Just one more," he said between clenched teeth.

"Sorry, old man, but when I agree to make a game the last, I stick to my agreement."

"But, but . . ."

Lord Baldwin picked up the paper on which Flavian had written, gave it another cursory look, then put it in his pocket. "I shall be happy to give you a few days to raise the money to pay for your house," he said. "If you cannot, then I shall be happy to relieve you of your house. My son has been looking for a place of his own, and I think Half Moon Street would suit him very well."

"How about another game?" Flavian asked, hating the pitiful, begging tone he was unable to keep out of his voice. "Tomorrow?"

"No, I think this will be my swan song at cards," Lord Baldwin said. "I think I shall try my luck at Newmarket next. Say, Curtis, what about you? Perhaps you would have more luck with horses?"

Sixteen

Selina looked at herself in the full length mirror on her wardrobe. She had on the water-green silk dress. She had decided to wear it for the portrait, not because it was the most beautiful and most expensive gown she owned—although it was—and not because she looked extraordinarily lovely in it—although she did—but because she already associated the gown with unhappy occasions, and what could be more unhappy than the occasion that was upcoming? In less than an hour, she would be in Carlton House having her portrait painted by a man she did not like at all, while attempting to become the mistress of another man whom she did not really know and, furthermore, did not want to know any better.

She remembered the night on which she had first worn the water-green silk, the night all her trouble had begun. She had been so happy then, so carefree. She had been a girl who was very much in love and who had thought she was loved in return. She had been looking forward to a

156

future unblemished by any worry more serious than which of several social engagements to give priority.

That girl no longer existed. Standing in front of the mirror now was a tired, careworn, dejected young woman who seemed to have aged years in a fortnight. At least, she felt as though she had aged. Standing perfectly still, she remembered how she had whirled about, looking at herself from every angle in her new gown, while downstairs Daisy and Flavian waited, almost as excited as she was.

Flavian—poor Flavian!—seemed to have aged centuries in the past twenty-four hours. He had gone out yesterday, and when he returned, he looked as though despair had found a home in his face. His shoulders sagged and he walked like an old, old man. She tried to find an opportunity to ask him what had happened, what catastrophe had now darkened their lives, but when she started to say something, he anticipated her and shook his head, indicating that he did not want to say anything in front of Daisy. She had not caught him alone since then so that she could ask, so she still had no idea what new and terrible news lurked in wait for her.

There was a light tap on the door of her bedchamber and Daisy came in. "Mr. Barelli has come," she said.

"Oh!" She had not realized it was time for him. He would arrive in the late morning, he had said, and she purposely had not looked at the clock. "I suppose this is it, then," she said. She gave her aunt a light embrace, as though she were about to set off on a journey.

"Selina," Daisy said, "even though you may have no heart for what you are about to do . . ."

"I have no stomach for it either, Aunt," she interrupted, thinking of the repugnant Prince.

"I was only going to say that right now, for a little while anyway, you won't have to think too much about him. Surely right in the beginning he will not . . . I mean, you can just concentrate on the honor of having your portrait painted by Barelli."

"Honor!" Selina spat the word out distastefully. "If this is an honor, I should hate to be dishonored!" Inwardly, however, she had to admit that Aldo Barelli was an exceptionally good artist and having him paint her was, indeed, an honor.

He was waiting for her at the foot of the stairs, a look of admiration in his eyes even though a slight frown was on his face. Obviously, he had no more enthusiasm for this venture than she.

He bowed to her and said, "We must go right along or we shall be late."

He was not one, she noted, for wasting time with idle compliments or social amenities.

Flavian and Daisy stood at the door as they left, and Flavian, as Selina went by him, whispered, "You *must* make a success of this, me gel, or all is lost. *All.*"

She nodded without responding and she and Aldo went out to the carriage. Neither of them spoke a word on the way to Carlton House. At one point, she chanced to glance at him and saw him looking at her questioningly, but she quickly looked away as though something was transpiring in the street which was of such importance that she had to give it her undivided attention. She did not look his way again.

They were expected at Carlton House. A footman in fancy livery bearing the royal crest met them and said, "Come with me, Miss Bryand, Mr. Barelli. Your studio is ready."

158

They were taken down a long corridor, through the gallery which Aldo had showed her the night of the party, and to a stairway behind the gallery. Upstairs, they went to the end of another corridor and the footman opened a door. "If you do not find everything you need, Mr. Barelli, just ring."

"Thank you," Aldo murmured as he and Selina went into the room provided as a "studio."

Selina gasped as soon as she looked around the room. It was a small sitting room, apparently quite near the Regent's apartment. It was almost as intimate, she thought, as though they were in a bedchamber!

Aldo, seeing the expression of horror on her face, said, "It is not too late for you to change your mind about having your portrait done. You can say you are feeling quite ill."

"I *am* feeling ill," she said, "but unless I have a fatal disease, this painting would only be postponed until I am in better health. Let us get on with it."

He helped her off with her pelisse and laid it across a chair. It appeared that everything he would need was already at hand: easel, canvas, pallette, brushes and oil paints. And in the center of the room was a dais on which sat a lacework iron chair containing bolts of different colored velvet.

"I assume the chair is to be partially draped with the color which goes best with your gown," Aldo said. "I think perhaps we shall use the blue. Blue and green together always have a sort of richness . . ."

"And that is what we want," Selina said, "richness."

He gave her a strange look as he helped her up to the chair. "The light could be better, but no matter. We will do the best we can with what has been provided. Now, will you sit back in the chair, please, and lean a little forward, just so . . . No, like this." He put one hand on the back of her head, the other on her chin, getting her face at just the angle he wanted. "Now, that is perfect. Will it be too uncomfortable a pose for you?"

"No," she said, "not if I am allowed to move a little every now and then."

He took off his coat. "Excuse me, but I find it impossible to paint in this. The sleeves hamper me."

"Quite all right," she said. With what was in store for her, who was she to be shocked by a man removing his coat in her presence?

But where was His Highness? She and Aldo were quite alone, not only in the room, but from the silence, she gathered they were alone in this part of Carlton House. She had thought the Prince would be sitting beside Aldo, leering at her all the while Aldo painted, and probably even making suggestions as to how the portrait was to be done.

She felt his absence almost as much as she would have felt his presence, but what she felt mostly was relief.

No sooner had the thought passed through her mind than the door was flung open and there he stood, the Prince in the flesh. In a great deal of flesh, she thought, then wondered why his obesity was always the first impression in her mind when she thought of him. If everyone else had the same reaction, it was no wonder that he was sensitive about his appearance.

"Barelli, my good friend, I had to come to give you my thanks for being so obliging," the Prince said (as though, Selina thought, he had not already told Aldo that he intended to sit and watch the "progress"). "Although," he added, "I cannot think that it is any great chore for one of your talent to paint one of Miss Bryand's beauty."

"Thank you, Your Highness," Aldo said, and Selina also murmured her thanks. "Miss Bryand is truly my most beautiful subject," Aldo added.

"Thank you, Mr. Barelli," Selina said, trying to smile, but thinking all the while that she would be more comfortable were she in darkest Africa being eaten by cannibals.

And that, she decided, was exactly how she felt: as though she were being eaten by two cannibals, albeit civilized ones who exuded charm when it suited their purposes.

The Prince walked up to her chair and stared at her with unblinking eyes, obstensibly scrutinizing her pose. He was, as usual, splendidly attired. He wore a black waistcoat and white pantaloons with black and white striped silk hose. A bit formal, Selina thought, for just after midday, but being the Prince, he could get away with wearing whatever he chose, she supposed. At one time it was rumored that Beau Brummel helped the Prince in his selection of clothes, but lately the Prince and Brummel had been on the outs, so apparently the Prince made his own decisions now, more was the pity.

When he had looked at her as long as good manners would allow, he walked over to the easel and stood behind Aldo, staring at what the artist was doing.

After a few minutes, he said, "Barelli, you must know that you do not have to paint *exactly* what you see before you."

"I do not understand, Your Highness," Aldo said, turning around and looking at the Prince.

"Do you not think she would be more enchanting if the gown . . . that is, if she were a bit more in *dishabille*?"

"More seductive looking, you mean," Aldo said, turning back to the canvas.

Selina felt herself reddening. They were discussing her as though she were a roast and they were trying to decide how she was to be carved.

"As you will," the Prince said. "What I had in mind was something like the women done by Boucher . . ."

"Surely you do not mean me to paint her as a nude, Your Highness!" Aldo put down his palette and brush.

"No!" Selina cried, standing up.

The Prince rushed to her and gently pushed her back into the chair. "Now, now," he said soothingly, "of course that was not what I meant. Carry on, Barelli—just as you were, if you think that is best."

Selina was relieved, but the relief was short-lived. After all, she thought, it is the result of these sittings that matters to him, not how the painting looks.

Aldo, however, did not carry on. He was looking almost as distraught at Selina. "Your Highness, she is out of position now. I shall have to rearrange her." He cleared his throat. "I do not want to seem presumptuous, Your Highness, but might I suggest that you would perhaps be happier with the painting if you waited until it is finished to view it?"

The Prince laughed, a not unpleasant laugh but one which bespoke comradely conniving between men. "Might I suggest, Barelli, that you listen to *my* suggestions?"

"But the painting is hardly more than a sketch at this point," Aldo said. He looked both unhappy and uncomfortable.

"Then I can assume that when it is finished, it will be

exactly what I want," Prinny said, still grinning at Aldo, and Selina would not have been surprised if he had winked at the artist to emphasize his meaning.

The Prince did not wink, though. He took a seat directly behind Aldo where he could see both the easel and the subject of the painting.

Selina's discomfiture grew until she was sure it must be visible not only on her face but also in the portrait. She kept wishing that Aldo would declare that they had done enough for one day and it was time to stop. She even toyed with the idea of faking a faint or a sudden attack of the vapors to call a halt to the sitting.

She did neither. It was Prinny himself who finally became restless and said to Aldo, "I think that is enough for today. We do not want to tire Miss Bryand, do we?"

Aldo looked almost grateful as he laid his brush down. "No, we most assuredly do not," he said. "Come, Selina." He picked up her pelisse from the chair.

The Prince took the pelisse from his hands. "You go along, Barelli," he said. "I will see that Miss Bryand gets safely to her own home . . . later."

With a sinking feeling, as though the world had come to an abrupt and sanguinary end, Selina realized that her life as a courtesan was about to begin.

Seventeen

Selina looked from one to the other of the two men while they eyed each other like wary dogs waiting to see which would be the first to growl and bare his teeth. It was obvious that Aldo had no knowledge of what Selina had in mind for the Prince, but he seemed to be all too sure of what was in Prinny's mind.

"Your Highness," he said finally, "since Miss Bryand came with me, I think I should escort her home. Also, there is no reason for you to have to send a carriage when I am going to Half Moon Street, anyway. It is right on my way. . . ."

"Is that where you live, Miss Bryand? Half Moon Street?" The Prince turned to Selina.

"Yes, Your Highness." Selina could not tell for sure, but she thought she might have gone up in his estimation a bit when he heard her address. Perhaps he would treat her more like a lady and less like a lightskirt or fancy woman when their affair actually began.

The Prince gave Aldo a benign look. "There is no reason for you to stay longer, Barelli. You and I are already acquainted. Now I want to become better acquainted with Miss Bryand since—" he pointed to the easel, "when you have finished, her portrait will hang in my best gallery."

There was no way Aldo could stall any longer. He had been dismissed, politely but firmly, by the Prince. He gave Selina a long, meaningful look and then reluctantly bid her and the Prince good day.

The look, Selina knew, meant that he wished he could help her, or that he could take her with him, but there was nothing he could do without openly defying the Regent which, of course, could result in anything from a disagreeable argument of a few minutes duration to imprisonment for treason or some other trumped-up charge. It was well known that the Prince could be charm itself or a fearful monster, depending upon whom he was with and which mood best suited his purposes.

No sooner had the door closed behind Aldo than the Prince turned to Selina, the smile she had come to dread engulfing his face.

He took a few steps toward her, then stopped, apparently seeing something in her face that put him off. "My dear," he said in a soft voice which oozed honey, "this is a rather uncomfortable little room, rigged up as it is right now for a studio. Let us go where we can be more comfortable as we become acquainted."

She would not have suspected the man with the reputation for being the most lecherous in all of England of being quite so obvious in his advances. Surely after having made a conquest of so many women—from scullery maids to titled ladies to royalty, if the rumors could be

165

believed (and she believed every one she had ever heard about him)—he would not be so gauche in his approach.

"This is quite comfortable, *very* comfortable indeed," she said quickly and, as if to emphasize her words, sat down in a small oak chair by the room's one window.

The smile never left his face, never changed. "How is it I had not seen you before the other night?" he asked, sitting down on the dais where she had posed for Aldo. It was with considerable difficulty that he lowered himself and, in different circumstances, she would have gone into a fit of laughter at the sight of this rotund man who tried to act as well as dress so much younger than he was.

"I have not lived in London long," she said. The urge to laugh had passed and she suddenly found herself quite touched. He was trying to be casual, to put her at ease with him, to make her like him. The fact that he was trying so hard to please made her think that he must be very unsure of himself. She had not imagined that either his dignity or his hauteur would bend in the slightest. She had thought that, without preliminaries of any kind, he would order her into his bedchamber as soon as he got rid of Aldo. But here he was like any young swain trying to press his suit with a belle whom he had just met. For the second time since she met him, she thought of him as a human being rather than as the Regent.

But a human being who wanted to seduce her! She must never lose sight of the reason the two of them were alone together in this small, intimate sitting room. For a moment she felt like the doomed Scheherazade and she wondered if she might interest the Prince in a series of stories to ward off seduction the way Scheherazade had done to ward off death. But to do so, she knew, would defeat her purpose. After all, she had come here to be

166

seduced, had she not? It seemed to her now that Flavian had been grooming her all of her life for this moment when she would become a mistress to the Regent.

The Prince leaned forward—not easy for him to do since his stomach was very much in the way—and took her hand. Without thinking, she almost withdrew it, but then she let it lie tranquil in his and even managed a sort of smile. If she was going to be a proper courtesan she must not appear unwilling, and certainly she must not even give a hint that she is repelled by her seducer.

The slight smile was all the encouragement the Prince needed. He began to pat her hand and then, before she was aware of what was happening, he pulled her from the chair to the dais beside him. *His* smile was now a mixture of grin and leer.

"I was sure you had not," he said.

She looked at him, perplexed. "Sure I had not what, Your Highness?" She regretted asking the question as soon as it was out. It should have been obvious to her what he meant; she not only had made a complete cake of herself, but also had given him a new and bawdy way of advancing the conversation.

"Sure you had not lived in London very long," he said mildly. "Our paths would have crossed before now. I would have seen to that." He took a lock of her hair between his fingers and said reverently, "You are truly glorious, an enchantress such as I have never seen before, the fairest lady in the land."

Inwardly, she shrank from his touch; outwardly, she continued to smile as she said, "Thank you, sire, and were I a scullery maid and not a lady, would you still call me glorious and an enchantress or merely a comely wench?"

167

He laughed, a little at first and then uproariously. "You say that as one who likes to jest."

"I would like to be court jester, Your Highness." She had no idea what possessed her to say such a thing—unless it was because she would say anything that came to mind to keep the conversation going. As soon as they stopped talking she would meet her fate as surely as Scheherazade would have met hers had the Sultan Schariar lost interest in her stories. She must, therefore, turn into a conversationalist of the first magnitude at once.

That thought left her frozen; she could not think of a single comment when he replied, "I think we shall find a better position for you at court."

Even her smile grew a little weaker at that remark.

"Come now," he said, and with a maximum effort pushed himself up from the dais. "I will show you the palace." He helped her up in spite of her not wanting to budge from the dais.

"I have seen Carlton House, Your Highness. Mr. Barelli showed me around the night I was here. It is quite lovely. Your taste is impeccable."

"Ah, yes, I remember your making a remark to that effect when we met," he said. "Well, my dear, I will show you places that Barelli did not, places that Barelli does not even know exist. Come."

She had no chance to do otherwise for he took her arm and steered her out of the little room and into the hallway as though she were a prisoner.

Which she was, she thought, albeit a willing one—or semi-willing.

He was as good as his word. He led her along the hallway showing her into bedchamber apartments that almost

168

made her gasp. There were giant beds with gold canopies, and chests and wardrobes of the finest wood containing exquisite carvings. There were antique draperies and tapestries done in gold and silver threads. There were gorgeous paintings and rare works of sculpture decorating every room.

She had always known that royalty lived extravagantly, but she had never thought about how extravagantly royalty slept.

During the time she had spent with the Prince since Aldo left, her mind had become so conditioned that she did not even find it odd that he was showing her only bedchambers.

"And now I shall show you my own rooms," he said, putting an arm around her waist as he took her back to the wide hallway. For the second time, she froze. She could think of nothing to say, and she would have been unable to move had he not propelled her along with his arm. As they approached a door more ornate than the others, he pulled her closer to him and kissed her cheek.

"You do like me, don't you, my lovely Selina?" He said it almost imploringly, and as though her opinion of him was tremendously important to him.

"Ye-es." It was no more than a whisper, but the best she could do. She was thinking of what lay on the other side of that horrid, ornate door. By the time she was again on this side, she would be the mistress of this strange, complex man. At this moment, her feelings about him were so contradictory that they all but canceled themselves out.

Both she and the Prince started violently at the sound of footsteps pounding down the hall. A footman was running toward them. "Your Hi . . ." he began, but he was

169

interrupted by a stream of the most scurrilous language Selina had ever heard. The Prince started out by calling the footman "a damned yellow dog of Satan," and went from there to much worse, ending finally with, "Everyone here knew I was not to be disturbed. You will be discharged. Now go before I take it into my head to squash you like the bug you are."

Abject with apologies, the footman was almost on his knees as he told the Prince that his father, the old King, was having another of his "spells" and was hallucinating badly. "He thinks the trees are ambassadors, and the doctor says the gout in his foot has gone to his head. The Queen wishes you to come at once, Your Highness."

There was a long silence and then the Regent said, "Oh. Well, then." That was as close as he came to an apology or to rescinding the discharge. He turned to Selina. "I must go, I am afraid. But we shall continue to get better acquainted some other time. Some time very soon."

She noticed that her hands were beginning to tremble at her narrow escape. It was only for the moment that she had escaped, she knew, but like Scheherazade, she had received a short reprieve. "Yes, Your Highness. I hope so," she managed to say.

To the footman, the Prince said, "See that Miss Bryand is taken to her home."

Eighteen

Feeling began to return to Selina while she was in the royal coach on her way home. It was then that she realized that she had been emotionally numb for the past few hours. It was as though she had been playacting in a farce, and now the play was over and she could resume her normal role in life. But only temporarily. She would have to return to Carlton House for Act Two, probably no later than tomorrow, depending, of course, upon the condition of the King.

King George had been in ill health for a long, long time, and rumors had been rampant throughout London that he had "spells" during which he was out of his mind. For that reason his son had become Regent. Today Selina had found out for a fact that the rumors were true. The King did, indeed, have "spells."

It was not likely that he would live much longer, and then the Regent would become King. And she would be the mistress of the King.

That thought reminded her of a story Flavian had told her once which she had thought funny at the time, but now she understood it better and the humor turned into one of those truths which hurt. A man who had displeased his fellow townsmen was tarred and feathered, put on a rail and taken out of town by four men. When he was dumped off the rail outside the town, he said, "If it hadn't been for the honor, I'd as soon have walked."

If if were not for the honor of being mistress to the Regent, she would as soon remain a vestal. And if there was humor to be found in that, she thought it rather grim humor.

For that matter, the whole situation struck her as being more than a little grim. The thought of having to return to Carlton House, of having to go inside that ornate door with the Prince, almost caused her to have an attack of nausea. Now that she was away from the scene, she could look back more objectively—and looking back, she knew she could never go through anything like that again. She knew now that during all the plotting and planning she and Flavian had done, she was able to go along with his ideas because none of them had seemed real to her. Flavian might as well have been telling her fairy tales which would never come true.

Now, after being faced with the reality of Flavian's plan, she understood for the first time just how much of her emotional as well as her physical self would be involved in carrying through those plans. She would never be able to do it.

She would never go back to Carlton House again, never pose again for Aldo Barelli to finish that horrid portrait which, without even having seen the bit of work he had done on it, she already hated with a passion.

172

What, then, would become of her—and of Daisy and Flavian?

She had long known that it would be up to her to bring the family out of whatever dire straits it was in—and from the look of Flavian for the past few days, it was apparent that something dreadful (even more dreadful than running out of money) had happened. His attack of the glooms seemed as though it might prove fatal unless she could come up with a cure. And, of course, the only cure was for her to come into a fortune quickly.

She discarded the Prince from her mind once and for all . . . and he was replaced almost immediately by a much more youthful, handsome, appealing and eligible man. Auberon Baldwin.

Even though she had not heard from him (and she had half expected that she would) since the night of the Carlton House squeeze, she knew that she had piqued his interest. Her eviction from Almack's was against her, but she thought she had explained that to him satisfactorily; and after having seen her at the Prince's residence, he certainly must know that she was acceptable among people of the first stare of elegance.

If she could arouse feelings of amour in the future King of England, surely she could do the same in a man of lesser importance. And this time her heart would be in her conquest for she found Auberon most attractive. It probably would not be too difficult, she thought, to come to love him.

As the royal coach turned into Half Moon Street, Selina's newest course of action was very clear to her. First, she would get to know Auberon better (in as little time as possible, for she was afraid there was little time left before the Curtises would be utterly bereft of money), and then she would get him to offer for her.

As the coachman helped her out, she saw and recognized a carriage in front of the house. Then she saw the owner of the carriage standing at the door, watching her alight. Even from this distance, she could see the expression, both worried and inquisitive, on Aldo Barelli's face.

She thanked the coachman, dismissed him, and went to the house, greeting Barelli with "I hardly expected to find you here waiting for me. Or were you calling upon my aunt and uncle?"

"There is no one home," he said. "Of course I am waiting for you. Why else would I be here? Are you all right? Did he . . ." He stopped suddenly, his voice breaking.

"I am quite all right, thank you. And no, he did not."

Aldo's face turned slightly red at her bluntness, but Selina herself was beyond blushing or feeling embarrassed. After her experience she felt more worldly than she had before—at least worldly enough to prefer frankness to masking reality with a veil of inanities.

"I was anxious about you," Aldo said.

"I appreciate your concern," she told him. Since no one was at home, she did not invite him in, nor did she want to. Now was the perfect time to tell him that she would be sitting for the portrait no more.

"I think you should know," she began, "that I shall not be going to Carlton House again. There will be no more sittings for the portrait."

He looked relieved. "I am glad of that. I think it was a mistake to do the painting in Carlton House. It is much

174

more difficult to paint—at least it is for me—with someone gawking over my shoulder."

"Then it is settled."

"Not quite," he said. "Will you reconsider and let me continue the portrait at my house, or even here at yours?"

"Certainly not!" she said emphatically.

"I should not ask this, but did something unpleasant happen to Carlton House to make you change your mind?"

"If you remember, I did not want my portrait painted in the first place. I have had enough—more than enough—of portraits."

She gave him a long, steady look, and when he did not reply, she went on, "As for what happened at Carlton House, or what did *not* happen, that is absolutely no concern of yours." She had no intention of telling anyone, except possibly to indicate to Flavian that there would be no liaison with the Prince.

"Sitting for a portrait is not the unpleasant task you seem to think it," Aldo said. "I assure you that if you were at Grosvenor Square it would be quite different from today."

"How can I make you understand that I do not want my portrait painted? I understand that I am in a small minority, that almost everyone in the world wants to be painted by Barelli, but please believe me, I do *not*!" She was tired and peevish and, however unjustly, was equating her bad experience today with this man who kept pestering her about her portrait. "I am not so vain as to think that posterity will be the better for having my likeness. Besides, I shall have no posterity!"

Aldo did not answer, but he gave her one of his enigmatic looks that made her long to know what he was thinking. She knew better than to ask, of course. She did, however, begin to wonder why he had been so much in evidence since that night when she had met him, the night she had gone to Grosvenor Square to meet Carlo's relatives. She had made no secret of her dislike for him since then, and his feeling for her—something akin to scorn, if she was any judge—was just as ill-concealed.

"I am quite tired," she said, dismissing him as easily as she had the Prince's coachman. "I am sorry I cannot invite you inside. Good day, Mr. Barelli."

He looked at her for a minute longer, his dark eyes piercing into her, and then he smiled, bowed, and without a word went to his carriage.

Daisy and Flavian had been walking in the park and when they returned they found, to their surprise, that Selina was already home. She had taken off the water-green silk and had put on an old French crepe. She was sitting in the bookroom, doing nothing more energetic than staring at the opposite wall.

Flavian's heart, which had been in his mouth all afternoon, suddenly stopped its wild palpitations and began to beat with a funereal kal-lump, kal-lump. It was obvious, to him anyway, that had Selina become the Regent's mistress (or even aroused his interest enough for him to want to spend a sociable hour or two with her), she would not have returned before nightfall. There was no need for him to ask her how her "sitting" went; he knew. Another disaster. How such a beautiful girl could fail so completely whenever a man was involved was something that was beyond his comprehension.

"Selina!" Daisy cried delightedly. "I am so glad you are

home. Was . . ." She started to ask a question, then stopped, not knowing how to word it delicately.

"I will tell you both this once, and then I do not wish to discuss the matter again—ever," Selina said. "I am not the Prince's mistress, nor will I ever be, nor do I have any desire to see him again. The truth is, I shall never make love with anyone whom I find repulsive, and I find His Royal Highness *very* repulsive. I would as soon have gone to bed with Henry the Eighth!"

With that, she left the room before either of them could say a word, leaving Flavian more than a little frustrated because of all the words he wanted to say.

That night, she relived the afternoon at Carlton House in her dreams. She was alone in the little room with Prinny, who was moving slowly toward her, that well-known lascivious gleam in his eye. She backed away from him, stepping around the dais, but he followed, knocking the easel off the dais in his eagerness to get to her. She reached the door and tried to turn the knob, but the knob would not turn. She had been locked in! There was no way now that she could escape.

Prinny caught her in his arms, holding her in a bear-like hug. She looked up at him to plead for her release and when she did, she realized that it was not the Prince who was holding her but Aldo Barelli. Before she could say a word, his mouth came down on hers and he was kissing her as she had never been kissed before.

She awoke suddenly, shivering—but neither from cold nor fear. She tried to go back to sleep, but found sleep impossible now. She was too engrossed in confusing new thoughts about Aldo.

Nineteen

In spite of fatigue after a restless night, Se-
lina was up early the next morning. She stood in front of
her wardrobe for a long time trying to decide which gown
would best suit her purposes. Finally, she chose a peach
muslin which was far from new, but still in style. Also it
was neither too drab nor too dressy for a walk in the
Park.

It had come to her during her wakeful hours that her
best chance of seeing Auberon quickly was to meet him
"accidentally" in the Park. She did not want to make an
appointment with him (though if she could not encounter
him any other way within the next few days, she would
have to resort to that), because she wanted their meeting
to look coincidental.

She was extremely careful, and took much longer than
usual with her toilette later in the morning. Even more so
than when dressing for Prinny, she wanted to look her
best, for this time she did not have the feeling of dread

and revulsion that had attended her last efforts at seduction.

"And what," she said to herself as she arranged her hair in a Greek knot on top with soft curls around her face, "if all of this is in vain? What if he is already involved with the girl Gemma and I saw walking with him in the Park?"

She did not think he was seriously encumbered with anyone, though. If he were, he would not have attended the Carlton House squeeze alone, nor would he have invited her to go in to supper with him.

She waited until late morning before leaving the house, and as she was going downstairs, she was stopped by Flavian. "Well, me gel, I gather you are not attired thusly to help your aunt with the washing."

"You gather correctly." She had neither the time nor the desire to talk right now. If Auberon were going to be in the Park, he would be there now—or in the afternoon. To be sure she did not miss him, she planned to stay most of the day. "I am on my way out," she told her uncle.

"And in a fierce hurry, I'd say." He made a great show of looking her up and down, then said, "Am I to understand that it is not the Prince who is claiming your attention and for whom you have rigged yourself up so?"

"You are to understand exactly that," she said. "I thought I had made that very clear yesterday."

"Ah yes, but you could have changed your mind overnight."

"That is something about which I shall *never* change my mind."

"Don't be too sure, me gel. We always end up doing the things we swear we will never do. I always said that I would never . . ."

But she had no time to listen. "Sorry, Uncle, I must go." She pushed past him and went down the rest of the stairs.

"At least tell me who the gentleman is you are meeting if it is not the Prince."

"I will tell you when I return," she said, hoping that she would indeed have something to tell him.

The Park looked lovelier than ever to her. The grass, which had lain brown and ugly for so long, was now all green, and flowers were bursting into bloom almost before her eyes. Had she not been on a mission of such importance, she would have liked to wander from path to path thinking about nothing, doing nothing but admiring nature. But she must stay away from the trails and walk along the roadside in case Auberon should be in a vehicle . . . if he came to the park.

After an hour of walking on first one road and then another, her optimism that he would appear began to sicken, and after the second hour, it died altogether. Although she had on her most comfortable slippers, her feet were beginning to tire and to ache. Not only that, but her pride was beginning to hurt also. That she should have to walk through the park for hours looking for a man made her, in her opinion, no better than the lightskirts who made a profession out of doing just that. The difference was, she supposed, that she was looking for one particular man and not just any man who came along. Had that been her goal, she could have succeeded already any number of times, for several men whom she had never seen before had bowed to her or smiled and indicated that they were far from averse to making her acquaintance. Furthermore, they were all gentlemen of quality from the looks of them.

Another half hour passed and she decided that she must go home. She would come back tomorrow.

It was just as she was leaving the park that a curricle stopped alongside her and Auberon's familiar voice said, "Good day, Miss Bryand. May I walk through the park with you?"

She was about to tell him that she would be delighted to have him walk through the park with her when something inside her cautioned her against being too available.

"I have had my walk, thank you. I was just on my way home."

"What a pity. I had hoped . . . Well, perhaps some other . . ."

Panic struck as she realized he was about to drive on. Quickly, she said, "However, if you would be so kind as to take me home, I should be eternally grateful. You see, I turned my foot on a stone in the path back there and it is paining me considerably."

He sprang from the curricle to her side immediately, telling her to lean upon him as he helped her in. As soon as she was settled, she said, "You are saving my life and I do thank you."

"I can think of no greater pleasure than saving your life," he replied lightly, "for that will make you enormously indebted to me. I shall insist upon payment, you know. And the price is that you go with me to Almack's next Wednesday night."

"And you shall receive your payment," she said, trying to match his lightheartedness while at the same time trying to think of something to say to extricate herself from the web she was already beginning to spin around them both. Obviously, she could never go into Almack's again. Was he inviting her merely as a test to find out? Deciding

181

that he was, she said, "I had already planned to go to Almack's on Wednesday. If you will be my escort, so much the better."

"With whom had you planned to go?"

"With Gemma Moraldo and her beau." She emphasized the word "beau" lest he should remember Gemma with more than casual interest.

"Shall we make it a foursome?" he asked.

"No, I think not," she said slowly, as though thinking through a weighty matter. "They are so much in love that I am sure they would rather go by themselves. They were merely being accommodating when they asked me to go with them."

"Very well," he said agreeably, "we shall go by *our*selves. Are *you* in love with anyone, Selina?"

The directness of the question startled her. She gave a little laugh, decided how she wanted to handle the situation, and said, "Why, sir, you are impertinent to the nth degree, but, no, I am not in love. However, there is someone for whom I think I am developing a *tendre*."

"Anyone I know?"

She nodded.

"Who is it?"

She smiled and lowered her eyes demurely.

His expression went from surprise to pleasure. "Do you like me, Selina?"

"Excessively." She made an extravagant gesture which seemed to take in all the world.

He laughed delightedly. "You are a flirt."

She became serious. "No, not at all." Unsmiling now, she looked into his eyes. "Sometimes people make jokes of the things about which they feel most deeply."

His eyes did not leave hers. He seemed to be trying to read something there.

"You look as though you are trying to read my mind," she commented.

"I only wish I could," he said. "I am trying to read the directions."

"Directions? What do you mean?"

"So I will know which way to go. I do not want to start off in the wrong direction."

"I still am not sure what you mean."

"This is Half Moon Street," he said. "You will have to tell me which is your house."

"The fourth on the left."

He stopped the curricle in front of the house. "May we just sit here and talk for a moment? I would like us to stop these infernal riddles and get a few things straight. Or is your foot paining you too much?"

"The first thing to get straight is what you mean about direction," she told him, ignoring his remark about her foot.

"All right, but first I would like to know what you meant when you spoke of joking of the things about which you feel most deeply."

She looked down at her hands, locked together in her lap. What had started as half game, half serious, was now all serious. "I think you know what I meant," she whispered. "I do not want to appear brazen or . . . or fast . . ." She stopped, unsure how to go on.

He took her hand. "And I think you know what I meant also. I think we may have started off in the wrong direction in the beginning—at Almack's—and the truth is, Selina, that since the first moment I saw you . . ."

He was interrupted by the opening of the front door and Daisy's voice calling, "Selina, is that you?"

"Yes, Aunt."

Daisy came out to the curricle, staring unabashedly at Auberon. "Wouldn't you and your friend like to come in?" she said, obviously giving Auberon her approval as a suitor for Selina.

Selina looked at Auberon and he nodded. "All right, Aunt," she said, and then she introduced Daisy to what she hoped would be Daisy's newest prospective nephew-in-law.

In the drawing room, Daisy said, "May I get you some tea, Mr. Baldwin, or would you prefer wine?"

"I think wine," he said. "It is more festive."

"A celebration?" Daisy looked hopefully from Selina to Auberon. "Perhaps we should wait for Flavian."

"Is he not here?" Selina asked.

"He went for a walk," Daisy said. "Actually, I think he went to look for you, Selina. You were gone for such a long time."

"Time passed faster than I realized," Selina said.

Daisy left the room to get the wine and Auberon went to stand beside Selina's chair. "I was about to say, before your aunt invited us inside, that since the first time I saw you I have been . . . very much attracted to you. I realize that I should not go about telling you in just this way, but I am a stranger to subtlety. I know I am much too blunt, but I have never been one for wasting time. I would like to have your uncle's permission to call upon you."

"But you are already calling upon me," she said.

"I mean formally," he said, "and if he wants to know my intentions, I wish to call upon you so that we may get to know one another and eventually . . ."

184

He left the rest unsaid, but she knew what he intended. She had not had such a joyous lift of spirits since the whole fol-de-rol about becoming Prinny's mistress began. There was just one problem: Eventually was not soon enough. Only Flavian could tell her how soon, but she was sure she needed to get an offer of marriage *very* soon. There was no time to be proper, no time to stand on ceremony.

"I would like that," she said. "I have found . . . have found myself quite . . . attracted to you, also."

He bent down and took her hand, "Oh, Selina . . ."

"I am blunt, too," she said, "and I know it does not become a lady. I should flirt with you and keep you wondering just what I think, but I find I cannot do that, Auberon. My feeling is . . . much too deep for that."

She need never worry again about what work she could do to earn a living, for now she was proving herself to be a very accomplished actress. (Not that she would ever need to worry about earning money now!) He actually was hanging on every word she murmured—not only that, but also *believing* every word. In a few minutes, she might even begin to believe too. She hoped she would, for to believe that she loved him would make the rest of her life much easier as well as much more enjoyable.

Daisy returned with a tray containing a decanter and two glasses. "Here we are," she said. "I hope you like claret, Mr. Baldwin. It was all I could find in the wine cellar."

The wine cellar, Selina knew, was a pantry behind the cook-room which had never at any time since she had lived here contained more than two bottles of wine at one time.

"Do we not have any Italian wine, Aunt?" Now why in

the name of heaven had she asked such an idiotish question? Italian wine—and Italians, for that matter—was the furtherest thing from her mind right now.

"Claret is just right," Auberon said agreeably. "Do you really prefer Italian wine, Selina?"

"Usually it is not as sweet as the French," she said, "and I do prefer dry wines."

Daisy gave her an odd look. "I did not know you were such a connoisseur of wine," she said.

"Are you not having any, Aunt?" Selina asked, wanting to change the subject.

"No, I have other things that need my attention and I am sure you two can do without my company," she said. "However, when Flavian comes in, perhaps we shall both join you."

"We shall look forward to it," Auberon said politely.

Beaming, Daisy left the room. Selina knew that her aunt was only slightly less happy than she herself at this moment.

"I like your aunt," Auberon said as soon as Daisy had left, "and I am sure I shall like your uncle. But most of all, I like you." He affixed a kiss on Selina's forehead, then sat down in a chair opposite hers so he could feast his eyes upon her. "I feel a trifle sad," he said.

Her heart sank. "Why, Auberon? Why should you feel sad?"

"Because of all the time we have wasted since we first met. By now we should be . . . practically engaged."

She laughed. "I thought we were . . . practically."

"What great fun you are!" he said, as though making an important discovery "I think we are alike in a good many ways, Selina. We seem to have several traits in common."

"Yes, I have noticed that." She would not disagree with him now if he said the moon was black and shone only at high noon.

"I must tell you," he said, "that for the past few months I have been looking for a house of my own. Now I should like to ask your help, because I shall not buy any house that does not please you."

Her cup not only was running over, but was spilling all over the floor and flooding the house. Regardless of whether she loved him passionately or only mildly liked him, looking for a house which would be her new home would be as heady an experience as she had ever had.

"I will help you gladly," she said.

She heard the front door open and Flavian come into the house, and she started to go to the entry hall to invite him in to meet Auberon, then changed her mind. It would be better for him to talk to Daisy first and let her tell him who was there . . . and why.

"Selina . . ." Auberon began hesitantly, "as you may have discerned, I am both impetuous and impulsive . . ."

"And you have seen that I am also," she interrupted.

". . . and I was wondering, do you . . . that is, wouldn't it be a grand surprise for our friends if we made an announcement next Wednesday night at Almack's?"

"What a perfectly splendid idea!" she cried excitedly while inwardly groaning. She would have to find last minute excuses for not going to Almack's until after they were safely married. When she became Mrs. Auberon Baldwin, she could go anywhere in London she chose without fear of being asked to leave or embarrassed in any way.

Her thoughts were interrupted by a knock at the front

187

door and, out of habit, she almost got up to answer before she remembered that Flavian was home now.

"That means," Auberon was saying, "that I shall have to speak to your uncle within the next day or two. You do think he will agree to our engagement, don't you, even though we haven't known each other very long?"

"I think so," she said. "I really think he will." Zounds! if only he knew how fast Flavian would agree!

"WHAT DO YOU MEAN, SIR?" From the entry hall came Flavian's voice, raised to a shout. "There was no time limit set."

She heard the voice of another man, replying, but she could not understand what was said.

"I will do no such thing." It was Flavian again, still shouting in anger.

This time both she and Auberon heard the reply. "My dear Mr. Curtis, you have no choice in the matter. In good faith, you made your own wager, and I, in good faith, accepted it. And now I have come to collect."

Auberon's ears pricked up. "That sounds like my father's voice," he said.

"Good God, man, how do you expect to collect a house?" Flavian asked. "You can't put it in your pocket like money and take it home."

"As far as I am concerned, that is exactly what this house is: money in my pocket," said the other man.

"That *is* my father," Auberon said, his face a study in shock. "What on earth is going on here? Are they . . ." He stopped to listen further to the conversation outside the door.

"I know your type," Flavian was saying. "You are just the kind who would put widows and orphans out in the snow. If you will just give me a little time, I will have the money for you, money enough to cover the house as well as the rest I owe you. I only need a month at the very most."

"I see no reason why I should extend the time. In a month you would be able to pay me no more than you are paying me right now. I have done some checking into your accounts, Mr. Curtis, and I found . . ."

"Three weeks," Flavian begged. "Just give me three weeks, Lord Baldwin, and I promise . . ."

"I will give you exactly a fortnight," His Lordship said. "At the end of that time I want the house and everything you owe me. Remember, a fortnight and not one minute longer."

Twenty

Selina sat as still as death. Not a muscle moved nor did her eyes blink. She could not believe what she was hearing, and yet she knew she was hearing correctly. Flavian had lost the house, an unspecified amount of money, and probably even the clothes he stood up in to Lord Baldwin in some kind of gambling deal. That certainly accounted for his long face of the past few days, his look of utter despondency, and his all-is-lost air. Literally, all *was* lost. It was obvious to her also that Daisy had not an inkling what was going on or she, too, would have looked as defeated as Flavian.

Suddenly she remembered with whom she was hearing the astounding conversation in the entry hall and she looked quickly at Auberon. He was leaning forward in his chair, probably the better to hear what was being said. But he was looking straight ahead of him, straight at her, and the look in his eyes almost made her shudder. He seemed to be accusing her, silently, of some terrible crime of which she had no knowledge.

She looked toward the door leading to the entry hall. The voices, quieter now, were continuing, but she could not hear what was being said. She looked again at Auberon and was overwhelmed by the change of expression on his face. He was looking back at her with complete contempt.

He continued to stare at her for what seemed an age before he said, "And to think I almost believed you! I almost tumbled right into your net of lies. To think I was making plans for . . ." He broke off as though so appalled at his own gullibility that he could not bear to mention it out loud.

"I didn't know," Selina whispered, close to tears. "I swear to you I did not know, Auberon."

He ignored her. "So you were developing a *tendre,* were you? You have found yourself quite attracted to me. Attracted to my money would be more like it! You are a scheming vixen, nothing but an adventuress, a fortune hunter . . ."

"Auberon, please listen to me," she implored. "You *must* believe me. I knew nothing about my uncle's gambling. I swear to you I didn't . . ."

". . . and we were going to have an announcement for our friends at Almack's next Wednesday night." He stood up suddenly, standing over her like an interrogator from the Inquisition. "I will wager a pretty penny myself that if you ever went back to Almack's you would not be allowed in. That was a Banbury tale you told me, wasn't it, about being mistaken for someone else? *You* were the one being asked to leave, and if you went back, you would be asked to leave again. Am I correct?"

She lowered her head and whispered, "Yes, but you do not understand. Please let me explain."

"There is nothing to explain. Everything is falling neatly into place now. And I must admit that you have been clever. You have made hardly any mistakes at all." He was pacing around the room now, looking over at her occasionally. "But tell me one thing. Did you think I would not know about your little scheme as soon as my father found out who you were? Did you think he would allow me to go on with marriage plans with you, knowing that you were only trying to pay your uncle's debts off now and probably in the future also?"

Tears coursed down her cheeks. "It wasn't that way at all," she said softly. "Auberon, I did not know your father had ever laid eyes on my uncle. You can ask my uncle. Wait!" An idea occurred to her. "Let's call them both in here, and then maybe we can straighten out this whole idiotish situation."

"Everything was just straightened out to my satisfaction," he said. "I am ready to take my departure—permanently."

She followed him to the door and out to the entry hall, still saying, "Please, Auberon, wait . . ."

At the front door, Lord Baldwin looked away from Flavian and at his son. "Auberon! Good God, what are you doing *here*?"

"I am just leaving, Father," Auberon said, complacency itself. "I have the curricle here, if you would care to join me."

"Here? Strange, I did not notice, but I had other things on my mind. I have my carriage, of course." Lord Baldwin's face still held a look of amazement. "But you did not answer my question. Why are you here?"

"Miss Bryand hurt her foot—or *claimed* that she did—while she was out walking and I brought her home." Auberon looked over his shoulder at Selina and nodded with satisfaction when she blushed at his use of the word claimed. "That was *all* I was doing here," he added.

"I am glad to hear that you were not paying a social call," Lord Baldwin said.

"Look here," Flavian piped up suddenly, a storm brewing on his face and in his voice, "you are to speak of my niece in nothing but respectful tones, you young whippersnapper, or I'll take a horsewhip to you!"

Lord Baldwin drew himself up like a peacock about to spread spectacular feathers. "You had better mind whom you are addressing, sir! Come, Auberon. It is beneath us to stand here arguing with the likes of these two. Far beneath us."

"You do not have to urge me twice, Father. I have discovered for myself *exactly* what these two are."

Baldwin *père* and Baldwin *fils,* their backs as stiff and straight as a stone wall, left the house and marched to the street like two soldiers who, having vanquished the enemy, were now going forth to collect their medals.

"You will be sorry for this," Flavian called to them. "You can't come here and insult me and my family. I will make you sorry for this."

As he got into his carriage, Lord Baldwin looked back toward the house. "Remember, Curtis, two weeks! Payment in two weeks!" With that, the carriage began rolling down the street, followed by Auberon in his curricle.

Flavian heaved a mighty sigh of frustration and exasperation. "Talking to a dolt like that is like spitting into the wind," he said bitterly. "It all flies back into your face."

Selina closed the door and faced Flavian. She was more angry and more hurt than she had ever been in her life, and she did not know whom to blame except herself for the lies she told and the schemes she had plotted—unless she could put at least a modicum of the blame on Flavian for forcing her into an untenable position. But she herself stood guilty as accused on every score but one: She had spoken truthfully when she had said she had not the faintest idea of what Flavian had been up to. She bared her teeth at him like a feisty dog about to attack. "How could you, Uncle? How *could* you?"

Flavian looked down the hallway, put his finger to his lips, and said, "Let us go into the bookroom. It is God's own miracle that Daisy didn't hear all the commotion."

Selina followed him into the bookroom and watched while Flavian sank exhaustedly into a chair. "I will repeat my question: How could you have gambled away *everything*? And what is to become of us now?"

"Now don't get your back up, me gel," Flavian said soothingly, attempting to shift the blame from himself. "After all, if you had been able to hold on to that young man . . ."

"I would have if you hadn't spoiled everything with your gambling!" She was almost shouting at him now. "He was already talking about offering for me and making an announcement!"

"Lower your voice, I said." Flavian eyed the door as though he expected Daisy to burst through momentarily. "He was, was he? Well, maybe not too much damage has been done. We can fix everything so . . ."

"You have already fixed everything, Uncle." Selina was becoming calm again with the hopelessness of the situation.

"Listen, me gel, when a young blade like that young Baldwin takes a fancy to a girl, it will take more than an uncle with a penchant for gambling to discourage him. I'll wager . . ."

"You've already wagered much too much," she interrupted. "Whatever possessed you to gamble away everything you have in the world?"

"You don't understand, Selina." He was almost like a child trying to explain some minor naughtiness to his mother. "I have always been lucky at cards before. Before Lord Baldwin came along, that is. Why, this very house in which we live was paid for by money I won at cards." He said it proudly.

"And now you have lost it the same way," she said. "I suppose that could be called justice of some kind, though I think it a pity that Daisy must suffer because of your trifling ways."

"Selina, I want you to promise me that you won't breathe a word of this to your aunt." Flavian looked as though he would have gone down on his knees to her if necessary. "It would break her heart. I will get it all back. I swear I will."

"How?" Selina asked disdainfully. "By gambling some more? Do you have anything left to lose, Uncle? If you have no collateral to back your wagers, I doubt if you will be too welcome in the gaming-hells."

"But if that young man wants to marry you, he surely is not going to let his father ruin it all for him by calling in his debts," Flavian argued.

"That young man has no intention of marrying me now. Now or ever." Selina fought to hold back her bitterness and her tears. "And I would not marry him now, knowing how little he thinks of me, with some reason, and of my family, with very good reason. Uncle, may I ask you just one question? Why did you not tell Aunt and me that you had gambled away the roof over our heads? Were you going to wait until we were thrown out into the streets for us to find out about it?"

"I will get it all back before the fortnight is up," he insisted. "I will get it all back."

"No," Selina said. "You would only lose more money that you don't have if you tried again. *I* will have to be the one to get it back."

With that, she left the room and went upstairs to her bedchamber. As she sat down at her little writing desk, she thought of the words Flavian had said to her only recently: *We always end up doing the things we swear we will never do.*

But she could not think about that now; she had to do that which must be done.

Taking out stationery, she penned a note to Aldo Barelli telling him that they would, after all, continue with her portrait, and that she was ready to resume sitting immediately . . . at Carlton House.

Twenty-one

When Selina went downstairs the following morning, she saw Flavian at the front door, and standing just beyond him was a footman in royal livery. She felt as though the world had dropped from beneath her feet and she was suspended in midair. So soon! She had not expected to have to resume sitting for the portrait for another day or two at least.

Flavian took something from the footman, closed the door and turned toward Selina. "A messenger from Carlton House," he said, handing her an envelope which bore the royal crest.

Numbly, she opened the envelope. The note, written by the Regent, stated that he wished her to go "for a little drive into the country" with him, and that the royal coach would come for her within the hour.

Without a word, she turned and went back above stairs to get ready for the "outing" in the country, knowing that this time there would be no reprieve. Today she would become the Prince's mistress, or, she thought, one of his many mistresses. If rumor could be believed, the Prince had as many mistresses as an Arabian sheikh had wives. However, he probably had favorites, and it was to be expected that the newest one would be his favorite.

The newest one surveyed her wardrobe and chose a lilac muslin, a rather prim little gown with a high neckline containing a touch of lace, and long sleeves with lace at the cuffs. It was the most conservative garment in her wardrobe. As she changed, her spirits were so low that she was afraid she would step on them.

Downstairs again, she told Flavian and Daisy what the note had said, and they inspected her as though she were about to assume a military command. Although Selina was not sure, she thought she detected a tear in Daisy's eye, while Flavian looked at her with open disapproval.

"What is this?" he asked. "The Prince invites you out and you dress as though you are in mourning!"

"This is hardly mourning attire," Selina said, "but I can assure you that if I had a black gown, I would consider this the proper time to wear it."

The royal coachman appeared at the door shortly, and without so much as a goodbye, Selina went with him to the coach. She was more than a little surprised, on being helped into the vehicle, to find it empty. She was the only passenger. Probably she was being taken to Carlton House and the Prince would get in then. She knew nothing about royal etiquette, but she assumed it was proper for her to be the one to have to wait upon the Prince rather than the other way around.

The coach did not go in the direction of Carlton House, though. It rattled along the streets at a steady clip and finally left the city altogether. Becoming more ner-

vous and more perplexed by the minute, Selina leaned
forward and called to the coachman, "Will you please tell
me where you are taking me?"

"To the country, Madam," was the instant reply.

"I can see that," she said, "but where in the country?"

For an answer, she heard the crack of the whip over
the horses' backs. Was it possible that the Regent had
merely sent his coach to take her for a ride?

Trying not to worry, she leaned back and looked at the
scenery. Flowers, both wild and cultivated, bloomed in
profusion everywhere; the forests were a deep, rich green,
and even the air, fresh and invigorating, bespoke the
height of springtime. Under different circumstances, she
could have enjoyed the ride very much, for she seldom
got a chance to leave the city.

The ride seemed a very long one, but she supposed that
was because of her anxiety and because time surely was
passing more slowly than she thought. It seemed much
later when the coach reached a tiny village, looking se-
rene and glisteningly clean in the midday sun.

She recognized the village at once. It was Windsor—
and there, overlooking the village like a mighty gray-
walled fortress, was Windsor Castle.

The Prince was having her taken to Windsor Castle,
away from the diverting interruptions of Carlton House,
away from any last-minute championing of her cause by
anyone (thought at this point she knew of no one who
would care whether she became the Prince's mistress, let
alone try to rescue her), and away from whatever
pressures the business of being Regent might force upon
him. They would be truly isolated in that vast fortress,
with only a few servants around to make sure their isola-
tion was not disturbed.

199

Selina remembered that the Prince had restored the castle which had been started by William the Conquerer, and had had the tower raised so that it dominated the entire countryside. Perhaps she could impress upon him her interest in seeing the restored castle and in that way stall off his romantic overtures. If he were as vain about the castle as he was about Carlton House, it would be a good ruse.

But no, what good would it do? Eventually, she would meet the same fate, and she was in no mood to be shown about a dank, drafty old castle, anyway. It would be better, she thought, to get it all over with and let the Prince send her home again.

The coach stopped in the courtyard behind the main bulwark of the castle and in front of that part of the gigantic structure in which the Prince had his private apartment.

She wondered how long she would have to wait at the castle before the Prince arrived. She hoped that it would not be a long wait, for she was anxious to be done with this whole sorry mess just as soon as possible and be on her way back to London.

The door of the coach was opened, and she held out her hand to be helped down by the coachman. As she stepped out and looked into the man's face, she had a sharp intake of breath. The coachman was standing beside the carriage, and it was Prinny himself who was helping her. There was a wide smile on his round face as he said, "Welcome to Windsor, Miss Bryand. I hope you will enjoy your stay here."

"I am sure I shall," she said, trying not to show either her surprise or her revulsion at the whole unsavory situation.

"You did not bring a traveling case with you?"

"I was not aware that I would be traveling, Your Highness. I thought I was going for a short drive into the country."

"And so you did go for a drive in the country." He was laughing at her. "I like to surprise people, put a little excitement into drab lives."

"I was not aware that I was leading a drab life," she said stiffly, forgetting in her anger that he was supposed to be addressed as Your Highness or another title of respect every time she spoke to him.

If he noticed her breach, he did not remark it. He seemed to be in an unusually good mood. "I am having us a bit to eat prepared," he said, "but I thought you would enjoy a walk about the grounds first after your ride from London."

"That would be very nice," she said.

His "walk about the grounds" consisted of nothing more than three turns around the small courtyard which they completed while she was still trying to think of some conversation.

"I trust the King is in better health today," she said finally.

"He is as well as he will ever be again in this world," the Prince told her. Then, as they completed the third turn, he said, "Now we can go inside," with a great deal of satisfaction, as though he had just completed a necessary but thoroughly unpleasant task.

Although she expected it, he did not mention showing her the restored castle. He took her firmly by the arm and guided her into a large drawing room which was part of his private apartment. A butler, a footman, and a serving

201

boy awaited them, standing beside a table laden with food.

The Prince's appearance and his penchant for women were not the only things he had in common with Henry the Eighth, she thought, as the footman seated her across from her host. The repast of which she was expected to partake consisted of a tureen of turtle soup, fillets of turbot, partridge and dried salmon, French beans and broiled mushrooms, and ended with a *gâteau millefleur*. She had never had such a feast laid before her in the early afternoon, but in spite of her hunger, she was of no mind to eat.

The Prince, however, seemed to enjoy his meal very much. He said little in the beginning, concentrating almost entirely on the food he had heaped upon his plate. But as his hunger diminished, he seemed to become aware once again of her presence.

"You must eat more," he said, giving her his ever-ready smile, "or you will blow away in the wind."

"I think there is little danger of that, Your Highness."

"No, I shall see that such a calamity does not befall you." He reached across the table and took her hand. "But before we go on to other things, do try a bit of this cake. It is delicious."

"Thank you, I believe not."

"Has no one told you that you are subject to the Regent? If your Regent commands, you are to obey." He said it with a gleam in his eye, but she suspected that he was not entirely making a jest. "Once you try the cake, you will want to go on eating it."

"Thank you, no," she said again. "I should not like to make a cake of myself."

He looked at her for a second or two and then laughed

heartily. "Ah, Selina, what a joy you are! Both to look at and to be with. And what a lucky day—or night—it was for me when Barelli brought you to Carlton House."

"Lucky for me also, Your Highness," she said in a tone scarcely audible.

He arose from the table and so, of course, she had to stand up also. He came around to her, again taking her arm, and said, "And now you shall see the rest of my royal rooms," and then he laughed as though he had made a great joke. His seeming reticence and shyness, she decided, were only noticeable when he was among a crowd. With a small group, or only one person, he was as bold as any brash young buck.

From the drawing-*cum*-dining room, he led her into an adjoining room which was not unlike the little sitting room in Carlton House in that it was small and gave the appearance of intimacy. The largest piece of furniture in the room was a huge red velvet couch, so large that it could have been mistaken for a bed.

Selina knew instantly that this was the room in which she would be seduced—or rather, the room in which she would have to submit willingly to the Regent. *If your Regent commands, you are to obey.* She closed her eyes for a moment, as though in prayer, but she could think of nothing to pray for, because this was something she had to go through regardless of everything. She opened her eyes again and looked into the eyes of the Regent.

Twenty-two

*For Selina, it was like having the same night-*mare twice. The only difference in the scene today and the one in Carlton House was the different setting. Otherwise, everything else was the same. The Prince was staring at her, his expression a cross between a leer and a look of hunger. She knew that, having just finished a gigantic meal, it was not food for which he hungered. Involuntarily, she drew back from him and said, "I have been told what a splendid resoration you have made of the castle. I would like to see what has been done."

She had thought she would not resort to stall tactics, that all she wanted was to get it over with, but now, at the last minute, she was willing to do anything to postpone the Prince's lovemaking.

"I shall be delighted to show you the entire castle . . . in a little while," he said, still eyeing her as though she were a golden roast duckling and he was about to have his first bite.

In a little while, she knew, would be too late. She looked hastily around the room to find some conversational piece, but the only thing that was the least bit different was that horrid red velvet couch.

The Prince, following her glance, also looked at the couch and then motioned her toward it. "Come, Selina, let us sit down here. This is my favorite room."

"Why is that, Your Highness?" Even on the edge of panic, she could not help but wonder why he of the elegant, extravagant tastes preferred this perfectly ordinary little room.

"Because there is nothing here that requires my attention," he said, "except the person I am with."

That made it fairly obvious that she was not the first person, the first woman, he had brought here.

"I see," she said, inadequately.

"And I am prepared to give you my full attention, Selina. For the rest of the day." He urged her down on the couch and then sat down beside her and encircled her waist with his arm. "There will not be any interruptions this time."

"How is the King?" She was struggling to keep a conversation going, saying the first thing that came into mind. "I trust he recovered from his . . , his attack." She did not want to say "spell," thereby insinuating that the King was, as everyone knew, as crazy as a bedlamite.

"You inquired about my father's health when we were outside," the Prince reminded her, "and I told you that he is as well as he can ever expect to be again."

"Oh, yes. I had forgotten. I am sorry."

"No need to apologize." His arm tightened around her and his face came close to hers. She could feel his breath on her cheek.

"Your Highness, I . . ."

"I think we may dispense with some of the formalities when we are alone like this, Selina."

At that moment, the sound of a great disturbance came from outside. Dogs were barking and the shouts of at least two men could be distinguished.

"What the devil?" The Prince got up and went to the window. "I told those idiots that . . ." He broke off as she joined him at the window.

Selina gasped, completely stunned by what she saw.

Outside in the courtyard, one of the Prince's guards was holding two barking dogs on a leash while another guard was struggling with—Selina could not believe her eyes—Aldo Barelli.

"That is Mr. Barelli!" she said in amazement, not even aware that she spoke out loud.

"I know it, and the devil take him!" The Prince's mellow mood had turned into a foul one. "What is that fellow doing here? Well, I suppose I shall have to find out. Sit down, my dear. I shall be back before you know I have gone."

But she did not sit down. She followed him out on the grounds to where Aldo was still struggling, though not as much because of threats to let the dogs loose.

"What *is* it?" the Prince demanded peevishly. "Why can't I have a little quiet, undisturbed . . ."

The dogs, their attention distracted from Aldo by the Prince, turned and began growling and then barking at His Royal Highness.

"Get them out of here," he shrieked, "and the two of you can report to the bailiff at once. You are dismissed!"

"But, Your Highness . . ." one of the guards began.

The Prince struck out at him, missed, then simply glared. "Go!" He pointed toward the rear of the castle.

The two men and the dogs left on the run. The Prince then turned his attention to Aldo.

"Barelli, what in the devil are you doing here?" he said, still unquestionably irritated, and it made him no happier when he realized that Selina had followed him outside and had witnessed the scene with the guards. "Surely you do not think Miss Bryand is going to sit for the portrait today, and *here*."

"I apologize, Your Highness," Aldo said, considerably calmer himself now that the dogs and the guards were gone, "but I felt it necessary to apprise you of . . ."

"Damn it, man, I cannot think of anything important enough that you should follow me to Windsor and disturb me here!"

Aldo was standing quite erect now, and his dark eyes were like black coals which smoldered underneath. "It is important to me and to Miss Bryand, Your Highness."

"Then say what you have to say and be off with you!" It seemed that the Prince's annoyance was to know no bounds.

"That is exactly what I anticipate doing," Aldo said. He made a slight bow in the direction of the Regent and said, "You see, Your Highness, I was not speaking truthfully when I told you that there is no relationship between Miss Bryand and me. She and I are . . . very close friends."

"The deuce you say! Are you trying to tell me that she is your mistress?"

Aldo did not confirm this verbally, but he looked at the ground, giving the impression that that was the correct interpretation of his statement.

Selina was too dumbfounded to do anything but gape at the two men who now stood glaring speechlessly at each other. Her first attitude was one of wild anger at Aldo. The absolute gall of that man! The very idea of his coming here and insinuating that she was his mistress! It was not to be believed nor tolerated!

She was about to make her sentiments on the subject known to them in no uncertain terms when she realized that even if she spoke, neither man would hear her. Although neither of them moved a muscle, their eyes were locked in combat. It was as though whichever could stare the other down would be the victor.

She looked at Aldo, his dark, enigmatic eyes telling her nothing. She could not even begin to guess what had possessed him to come here today and lie to the Regent about her being his mistress—even though only by insinuation. If it were not such an appalling lie, it would be downright funny.

His stance and his expression told her nothing either. It dawned on her suddenly that if she knew Aldo for a lifetime, she still would have no idea what the man was thinking.

She looked at the Prince then, and though he was far from a transparent man, beside Aldo he seemed readable. She was *almost* sure she knew what he was thinking as he tried to win in this strange battle of stares.

He was thinking—she was positive—that Aldo was not one of his subjects whom he could order around at will. Aldo was a foreigner, and a very noted one at that. It was, in fact, Aldo Barelli, the celebrated artist, whom the Prince wanted to paint his portrait—as well as that of the woman he planned to make his mistress. He could not afford to antagonize him or Aldo might refuse to paint the official portrait.

Apparently, her surmisal of his thoughts was not incorrect, for the Prince gave up and lowered his eyes, then turned suddenly to Selina and said, "All right, go with him. I cannot keep you here if I expect him to do a good likeness of me—and I *do* expect it, Barelli, a *very* good likeness of me in the portrait you are going to paint."

It was obvious to both Selina and Aldo that the Regent's unspoken message was: It is easier to find a beautiful, available woman than it is to find a superb, available portraitist.

A slight smile played about Aldo's lips, though his eyes still had a somber look. "You will get it, Your Highness. You will get the best likeness I can paint."

He walked over to Selina, then gave her his arm. "Come, Selina, we must be getting back to London."

Selina looked again at the Prince, half expecting him to protest, but he said not a word. She glanced back at him again as she and Aldo walked through the courtyard and he was standing in the same spot, his face like that of a pouting child with lower lip dropped. As soon as they were out of sight, she was sure that he would throw a childish tantrum.

Aldo had left his carriage a good distance from the castle. It was at the foot of the hill on which the castle sat like an ornament on the topping of a cake.

Neither of them spoke until they were in the carriage, and then Selina lashed out at him. "You are an unprincipled, lying beast!" She was quivering with anger.

"Lower your voice, my dear," Aldo said, "or my driver may get the wrong impression of what is going on."

She wanted to hit him. He had exasperated her beyond

words now, and the only thing left was to strike out at him with all her strength. She raised her hand, then decided that it would be but a futile gesture, so she lowered it to her lap again.

He was looking at her as though he did not understand why she was so furious. "Selina, do you not know what was about to happen there? The good Prinny was about to . . ." He paused, as though in deference to her delicacy, then said, "You may thank me any time now for rescuing you from the clutches—literally, I have no doubt—of that mendacious Lothario."

That was the terminal stalk of grain!

"You must be mush-brained!" she cried. "You have ruined everything for me, *everything*! I was trying to become the Regent's mistress. Can't you understand anything? I *wanted* to be his mistress!"

"I do not believe that for an instant," he said complacently, ignoring the invectives she hurled at him. "I do not believe my judgment of you is so mistaken."

There was no point in trying to think of more vitriolic words to say to him; the episode was over. The whole sordid, though brief, affair had ended. Never again would she have another opportunity to become the mistress of the Prince, for he would always think of her as Barelli's mistress. No matter which way she turned, there was nothing but defeat, and she had better learn to accept it, to live with it.

Resignedly, she turned to Aldo and said, "How did you know where to find me? Even I did not know where I was being taken when the coach came for me."

"When I received your note saying you wanted to continue with the portrait at Carlton House, I went to your home to see why you had changed your mind so abruptly," he said. "I was very much of the opinion that you had no desire to sit for the portrait ever again, and most certainly not with the Prince present."

"You assumed too much, sir," she said coldly.

"When I got to Half Moon Street, I saw you being helped into the royal coach," he said. "I followed the coach to Windsor."

"So you did," she said, her voice dripping sarcasm. "You must have arrived shortly after the Prince and I did, so if you were coming on the errand of mercy you claim, why did you delay so long in your rescue?"

"It took me a long time to get to the courtyard," he said. "When the Prince is in residence, the guard around the castle is tripled. I finally managed to talk myself as far as the courtyard by telling them that the Prince had sent for me because he wanted me to continue painting the portrait of the young lady who was with him. The two guards in the courtyard did not believe me, however, for the Prince himself had told them that he was not to be disturbed. I had just begun to try to fight my way into the castle when the Prince came rushing out."

"You are lucky that you were not devoured by the dogs," she said.

"Now, Selina, will you please explain to me why you seem to be trying so hard to become the Regent's doxy?" he asked. "And do not give me any more of this fustian talk about wanting to!"

Selina sighed. Now that it was all over, she might as well be honest with Aldo. After all, at considerable risk—possibly even to his life—he had rescued her from the Regent and, in spite of the fact that she had been about to succeed in her endeavors, she would have to admit both to herself and to him that she was more than delighted at being saved from that amorous mass of whale blubber.

Se she poured out the whole story to him from the beginning, and it almost amounted to a recital of her life's history from the time she came to London until she learned that the Curtises needed money, and then extending to Flavian's perfidy in losing the house and every last penny of his money.

Strangely, as she talked, she did not see the sympathetic expression on his face that she expected. He seemed to be having considerable difficulty holding back his annoyance.

His attitude, even though it was unexpressed, caused her anger to rise again. And after she finished her story and he said, "Why did you not come to me for the money? I would have given it to you. I will give it to you now," she wanted to snap at him like a young puppy.

"I did not go to you for money because I am no more desirous of becoming your mistress than I was of becoming the Regent's," she said heatedly.

"I should not insist upon such collateral," he said, giving her a stony look.

They rode the rest of the way to London in strained, unfriendly silence.

Twenty-three

If the ride to Windsor had seemed long, the ride back to Half Moon Street was twice as long. With every turn of the wheels, every jostle of the carriage, Selina became more uncomfortable, not physically so much as mentally. Sitting so close to Aldo Barelli that their bodies almost touched, she felt strange. She felt that she suddenly did not know herself any better than she knew him, and a great wave of sadness swept over her at the thought that she might never know either of them any better than she did right now. And this, in itself, was inexplicable. Why, in heaven's name, should she want to know Aldo Barelli any better? He had brought her nothing but misery since the first minute she set eyes on him the night she had gone to Grosvenor Square with Carlo to meet Aldo and Gemma. Carlo. He seemed now like someone she had known eons ago and, looking back now, she realized that she had never loved him at all. She had been in love with the idea of being in love, in love with the idea of being

Mrs. Carlo Moraldo. And then her troubles had started when she met Aldo . . .

No, she told herself immediately, all her troubles could not be blamed on Aldo. It was not his fault that his nephew had been a spineless coward, nor was it his fault that Flavian had gambled away everything he had, nor was it his fault that she had made a fool of herself by trying to become the Regent's mistress. In truth, the only thing she could blame him for was the fact that she had *not* become the Regent's mistress.

Out of the corner of her eye, she studied his profile. He not only had a handsome face, but also a strong one. There was nothing of his nephew's qualities in him. Regardless of how much she detested Aldo, she could admit to herself (but never to him) that he was, indeed, of sterling character, and had she met him under different circumstances she probably would have liked him.

Without warning, the dream she had had about him came back to her, the dream in which he had been about to make love to her and she had awakened feeling a thrill going through her. Inadvertently, she wondered what it would be like to have Aldo make love to her and, looking at him again, she could feel herself blushing. What a mercy that he could not read her thoughts!

She did wish that the two of them could have kept up some semblance of a conversation on the way back to London. It would have made the journey less dull and the time would have passed more quickly. But try as she would, she could think of absolutely nothing to say to him—and it was quite obvious that he had nothing more to say to her.

Finally, they were on Half Moon Street, and the carriage stopped in front of the Curtis house, soon to be the Baldwin house.

As unexpected as a sudden, blinding flash of lightning, Aldo took her in his arms and kissed her soundly on the mouth. It was a full minute before she regained presence of mind enough to struggle against him.

"Stop that," he said softly. "You know you love me—almost as much as I love you. And I have loved you from the very first."

"I most assuredly do *not* love . . ." she began, then stopped. She could not tell him that she did not love him. For some reason, she could not get the words out. Then she realized why: she *did* love him!

Was it possible? she asked herself. Could she really love this man whom she had claimed to hate for so long?

Not only was it possible, it was a fact. She loved him very much, probably had for a long time, but would not admit it to herself. And what was that he had just said to her? He had loved her from the very first.

"I do not propose to spend the rest of my life following you around to snatch you out of the arms of other men, not even the ruler of the country," Aldo said, "Therefore, what I do propose is that you marry me."

The thought of loving him was still too new; she could not quite take it in yet. "I cannot marry you," she said. "There is the matter of Flavian's debts, and I will not hear of your paying them."

"I am a wretched gambler," he said. "I always lose—so you might hear that I have lost to your uncle."

"No, I will not let you do that, either," she said. "It would not be fair to you."

As he handed her out of the carriage, he said to her, "I think I shall be the one to decide what is fair and what is unfair. After all, I have waited long enough for that privilege."

At that moment, she saw Flavian coming down the street in a gait that was almost like a child skipping. Even before he was close enough to speak, she knew that he was euphoric. When he did speak, he did not greet them, but said at once, "Everything is all right again! We do not have to worry any more."

"What is all right, Uncle?" Selina asked. She knew that Lord Baldwin would never forgive the debts, yet she could think of no other reason for Flavian to declare everything all right.

Flavian looked toward the house. "Do not tell Daisy, please, but I have just been to a gaming house—not the one where I lost to Lord Baldwin—and I have won almost enough to pay him. I have enough to buy back the house, and one more day of cards should pay the rest of it."

"Thank heaven!" Selina exclaimed, so pleased at the results of Flavian's gambling that she forgot to scold him for going back. "But, Uncle, I want you to give me your word that you will not go back. You could lose the house again and then we would be right back in the same sorry fix all over again."

"But, Selina, I must . . ." Flavian began.

Aldo spoke quickly. "Mr. Curtis, I would like to challenge you to a game of cards of your choice, after which I have a matter of some urgency on which I wish to speak to you." Aldo gave Selina a knowing look, and there was no doubt in her mind as to what that "matter of some urgency" was. He was going to offer for her.

Flavian's eyes lit up. "Which gaming-hell do you prefer?"

"If you have cards, why do we not just go in your house right now?" Aldo said. "Surely your wife would not object to a friendly little game. She need not know that there is anything at stake."

"Perfect!" Flavian said, and in that one word, he included the entire state of his world at this moment.

Taking Selina aside, Aldo said, "While I am joyfully losing a little money, why do you not go in my carriage to Grosvenor Square and tell Gemma that she is to have you as an aunt instead of a sister-in-law?"

Just picturing the expression on Gemma's face at hearing such astounding news made Selina burst into peals of laughter.

The butler opened the door for her, bowed and stood aside for her to enter. It was almost as though he expected her, but Selina knew that this was not possible.

"Is Miss Moraldo in?" she asked.

"I will get her."

Selina waited in the elegant entry hall. In her state of excitement, she had not looked around the rotunda, but when she did, she gasped, then put her hand over her mouth to keep from crying out.

In the most prominent place in the hall, in the curve of the stairway which faced the front door, was a portrait of herself.

But it could not be, she thought. Her eyes were playing tricks upon her. She had sat for no such painting.

She went over to the wall and stared. There was no question, it was indisputably herself at whom she stared, lustrous brown hair, brown eyes which looked as alive and shining as the real ones, delicate ivory tones on the flawless skin—there was one thing about the painting which was undeniably clear: it showed the unmistakeable love of the artist for his subject!

However, the Selina in the elegant gold frame had on a white gown that looked not unlike a wedding gown. She had never worn such a garment in Aldo's presence, indeed, had never even owned anything similar to that stunning, regal-looking gown.

There were so many questions in her mind about the portrait that she could hardly look at it without thinking in questions, and yet, it was such a beautiful painting that she could not take her eyes from it. The Selina in the portrait looked very much the way the real Selina had been feeling for only the past hour: at peace with herself and the world, serenely, supremely happy.

"So you are finally seeing it," said a voice behind her. "It is the ultimate in magnificence, isn't it?"

She whirled around. "Gemma! How? When?" She could not even pretend to get all the questions out at once.

Gemma laughed. "Aldo began painting it the day after you first came here. I happened to go to his studio the next morning and he was already at work on it."

"But I never sat for him. Not then, anyway."

"He didn't need you to. You were perfectly etched in his mind. In fact, I think he memorized you the instant he set eyes upon you."

"But why did he do it? I was . . . was engaged to Carlo."

"No, Aldo knew even before he met you that you and Carlo could never marry," Gemma said. "And then after he met you, he knew that he himself was going to marry you. He was like a man possessed, Selina. I longed to tell you, but I knew I couldn't as long as you felt the way you

218

did about him. Although," she added with a grin, "I don't think you disliked him half as much as you pretended."

"That white gown," Selina pointed out, "it looks like a wedding gown."

"It is," Gemma said. "Aldo said that was the way you would look on the day he married you. He said that was to be your official wedding portrait. And, in case you are wondering, he will get a *modiste* to make you a gown exactly like the one in the painting."

Words failed Selina. She could only look from the portrait to Gemma and then back to the portrait again.

"He finished it yesterday," Gemma said. "I had not expected you to come to see it quite so soon."

Selina began to laugh. "Gemma, I thought I had some startling news for you, but it is you who had the news for me. What I have to tell you will not be in the least surprising now."

"Tell! Tell!"

"Aldo is with my uncle right now, offering for me." She saw no reason to burden Gemma with the knowledge that the offer would follow a card game.

Gemma clapped her hands. "Oh, Selina, I could not be happier! Just think, I will have an aunt who is only two years older than I, and one who is my closest friend." She hugged Selina. "But how did you get here if Aldo is with your uncle?"

"He told me to come ahead, and then I sent the carriage back to wait for him."

Even as she said it, her heart began to pound knowing that he would arrive soon and tell her that all was well, that they could begin to plan their marriage.

She pictured the way he would look when he came through the front door, the expression of joy and antici-

pation on his face. She was determined that when he
came in, he would see her standing beside the portrait:
the Selina he had painted adoringly, the vision of his love,
and the real Selina who returned his love so completely
that it could be captured on no canvas.

MASTER NOVELISTS

CHESAPEAKE·
CB 24163 $3.95
by James A. Michener

An enthralling historical saga. It gives the account of different generations and races of American families who struggled, invented, endured and triumphed on Maryland's Chesapeake Bay. It is the first work of fiction in ten years to be first on *The New York Times Best Seller List.*

THE BEST PLACE TO BE
PB 04024 $2.50
by Helen Van Slyke

Sheila Callaghan's husband suddenly died, her children are grown, independent and troubled, the men she meets expect an easy kind of woman. Is there a place of comfort? a place for strength against an aching void? A novel for every woman who has ever loved.

ONE FEARFUL YELLOW EYE
GB 14146 $1.95
by John D. MacDonald

Dr. Fortner Geis relinquishes $600,000 to someone that no one knows. Who knows his reasons? There is a history of threats which Travis McGee exposes. But why does the full explanation live behind the eerie yellow eye of a mutilated corpse?

8002

GREAT ROMANTIC NOVELS

SISTERS AND STRANGERS PB 04445 $2.50
by Helen Van Slyke
    Three women—three sisters each grown into an independent lifestyle—now are three strangers who reunite to find that their intimate feelings and perilous fates are entwined

THE SUMMER OF THE SPANISH WOMAN
                                CB 23809 $2.50
by Catherine Gaskin
    A young, fervent Irish beauty is alone. The only man she ever loved is lost as is the ancient family estate. She flees to Spain. There she unexpectedly discovers the simmering secrets of her wretched past . . . meets the Spanish Woman . . . and plots revenge.

THE CURSE OF THE KINGS CB 23284 $1.95
by Victoria Holt
    This is Victoria Holt's most exotic novel! It is a story of romance when Judith marries Tybalt, the young archeologist, and they set out to explore the Pharaohs' tombs on their honeymoon. But the tombs are cursed . . . two archeologists have already died mysteriously.

8000